Groupie Love

(A Heart Light Romance)

JENNIFER LEE BURNS

authorHOUSE®

AuthorHouse™
1663 Liberty Drive
Bloomington, IN 47403
www.authorhouse.com
Phone: 833-262-8899

Published by AuthorHouse 04/18/2023

ISBN: 979-8-8230-0586-9 (sc)
ISBN: 979-8-8230-0585-2 (e)

Library of Congress Control Number: 2023906771

Print information available on the last page.

Dedications

This book is dedicated to the hard-working entertainers and frontline workers, and to the many people behind the scenes it takes to get them ready or to get them to where they are supposed to be. Whatever it is that keeps you away from home, on the road, or away from your families... know the fans are extremely grateful for your many sacrifices. Be safe!

And to my best friendly! I could not have done this without you. We've traveled many miles making memories with our boys. This book is dedicated to you too! Thank you for sharing such wonderful times with me!

Chapter One

The band Dillonsledge was staying in town tonight because they finally had a much-needed day off. While backstage before the concert, band members Donovan and Derek had invited their favorite fans back to the hotel after the concert. Allison and Madison were full of nerves, but excitement won the battle for a resounding yes. They would soon be spending their first evening with their all-time favorite persons in the world, (except for each other, of course!)

Allison and Madison hurried back to their hotel after the concert to freshen up and prepared for a 'sleep-over' with their favorite band members… just in case! They emptied things from their purses they would not need in order to make room for things that might come in handy that night… just in case!

It was an unusually quiet ride to the hotel to see the boys. Allison parked the car and took a long breath before opening her door.

"Are you having doubts about going in?" Madison had gotten out of the car and opened Allison's door for her.

"Not really, more like fear! I don't want it to change

anything. You and I know we'll be fine after the fact, no matter what happens... we'll go back to our ordinary lives, gladly, and then after the concert in Atlanta, we probably won't see them until the next album comes out. Will the boys still be glad to see us the next time, and the time after that? So many people expect things from them. I don't want them to think we're using them, or that we'll suddenly expect more. I would rather not sleep with Donovan and still be friends, than have a one-night stand and lose what we have now."

"I'm willing to take that chance! And I know you are too. So come on! Live for 'right now' for a change and quit worrying about the future. Because right now, they are up there, and they are waiting... for us!" Madison turned pointing. She was right. They were about to have the chance of a lifetime, the chance to do something not very many people could say they had gotten to do...and she was not going to blow it worrying about what might, or might not happen, or if there would be a next time.

They made their way to the lobby and called up to let the boys know they had arrived. Derek said he would meet them at the back elevators and was already waiting when the girls got there. "It's about time. What took you so long?"

"Hey! We got here as soon as we could. Turn here, take that hallway there, it's like a maze in this place." Madison's mouth was watering. She swallowed really hard trying to suppress her nerves.

Allison laughed, knowing her best friend was suddenly feeling the same thing she had felt earlier in the car. Derek stuck his key card in the slot and pushed the button for the fourth floor, then turned and gave the girls a big hug, like he was genuinely glad to see them.

When the elevator door opened, Allison hesitated again for just a brief second! Two years following their favorite band... seven concerts total so far, five with their heart light keychains, backstage passes, talking on the phone with Donovan more and more all the time, and now they were going to the boy's hotel room. Allison could not believe how things had progressed. Never in a million years did she imagine getting to meet them, much less hanging out with them... or sex. Allison's thoughts were quickly interrupted.

"Hey! Are you coming?" Madison grabbed Allison's arm. "Come on!" Allison changed her thought process as she entered the somewhat plush hotel room, which wasn't really any better than the hotel she and Madison had splurged for during their very first concert two years ago. She decided she didn't have anything to be worried about, after all the boys had invited them. It's not like they were just hanging out in the lobby or showed up at their door unexpectedly!

Worry was quickly replaced by anxiety when Donovan came out of his room putting his shirt on. His hair was still wet from the shower, and he had that fresh, clean smell; much better than the smell backstage after some of the concerts. He hugged Madison and kissed Allison on the cheek, waving his hand towards the sofa. "Sit down and get comfortable. The pizza should be here shortly."

Allison sat down on the end of the couch pulling Madison down to the middle beside her; so, Donovan sat in the chair beside the couch on Allison's side. Derek plopped himself down beside Madison, putting his arm around her on the back of the couch, and his sock covered feet up on the coffee table in front of them.

Without even thinking Madison pushed his feet off the coffee table. "Don't put your feet up there. That is probably where we are going to put the pizza!"

Donovan was the only one laughing. Everyone else was in shock, including Madison, who could not believe she had just done that! She finally giggled, thinking Allison couldn't reach him, or she would have done the same thing. Allison laughed at the same time. "I know. I couldn't reach him!" And to think, the girls were worried about being able to be themselves around the boys when they first started hanging out with them, and now they were slapping them around.

Conversation was typical following a concert, until the front desk called to let them know the bellhop was on his way with their pizza. Donovan grabbed several beers from the fridge. "Does everyone want a beer?"

"Not me, I'm driving." Allison did not drink very often, and definitely not when she was driving!

Donovan handed two beers to Derek, one for him and one for Madison. He leaned over the couch, whispering in Allison's ear. "I was kind of hoping you wouldn't be driving back tonight." He held the beer out for her to accept. His soft seductive voice tingled in her ear, and the heat from his warm breath sent shivers through her entire body.

Knowing full well what he meant, she reached up and took the beer, teasing. "So, you guys are going to share a room, and give Madi and I the other room tonight?"

Derek perked up. "What?" Madison shook her head, patting Derek's leg, then rubbing it back and forth, getting a little higher each time. "Don't worry! She is only kidding. If I am staying here tonight, it won't be with her!"

Allison had no intention of staying with Madison either. She finished her pizza and her beer, and since the invitation had been given, she was more than ready to officially accept. Allison leaned back, looking straight at Donovan. "Well, I'm extremely tired, and now I can't drive."

Donovan almost choked. "And I'm suddenly full!" He stood up, laying the rest of his piece of pizza back in the box, taking Allison by the hand. "I guess we'll see you guys in the morning."

Madison turned to Derek. "So how full are you?"

He jumped up right away. "Full enough for now!"

The following morning, they ordered room service and lounged around until the boys had to get ready to leave. They had radio interviews, and commercials to make before heading up the coast. Donovan promised Allison he'd call as much as he could. He acted worse than she did about having to part separate ways, clinging to her, pouting. Allison wasn't sure, but thought Donovan would have taken her with him to the next concert, if she had wanted to go.

Good thing he didn't ask, or she would have turned him down. She had a life to get back to, a very ordinary life compared to Donovan's, but it was hers and at least for the time being, she liked it. Allison and Madison drove back to their hotel to check out. Donovan had already called, saying how much he missed her.

"OMG! What did you do to that boy last night?" Madison teased her, batting her eyes, moving her hand up to her forehead like she was going to pass out.

"So how was your Dillon Sledge concert last night?" As they were putting their bags in the car, a couple they met the day before was leaving for lunch and noticed the girls packing up to go home. The couple had stopped at the back door of the girl's car. "It's not Dillon Sledge, honey. It's Dillon's Ledge." The wife was quick to correct her oblivious husband.

The girls laughed. "The concert was amazing." Madison calmly pronounced.

"As usual!" Allison added. "They always do a good job."

This confused the husband. "Then shouldn't you be talking a mile a minute and squealing in extremely high octaves?" He squeaked in a hurried, high-pitched voice.

The girls laughed. Allison asked him how many daughters they had. "We have two girls." He said. "And a boy! And even Frank Jr. has a tendency to get overly excited at events." His wife added. "Well, it was nice to meet you girls. Have a safe trip home, and be careful."

In usual fashion, the girls jabbered all the way home, remembering as much about each of the concerts as they could. Their first Dillonsledge concert completely blew them away, seeing the band in person, seeing the boys up that close, nearly passing out when Donovan and Derek waved at them. They had barely recovered before the second concert when they won tickets to go backstage before the concert. Meeting Donovan and Derek was not something the girls ever thought would happen. Getting seats that close to the stage for both concerts was a rarity in concert going. You might get lucky once, but two concerts in a row were unheard of, unless you had connections, which they didn't have. Then being pointed out of the crowd during their first concert, and tickets to meet the band backstage during their second concert; that left them wondering what the rest of this tour had in store.

Allison was shocked when Donovan asked for her number that night backstage before the second concert, and even more so when he actually used it to call her the next day, and the next day. By their third concert, which didn't happen until the next album came out, Madison had found some key-rings with heart shaped lights attached. The whole heart lit up, with a bright light at the end, a flashlight. She got one for herself and one for Allison. They took them to the concert and held their hearts up for the boys to see. After the fourth concert, Donovan caught Allison off guard backstage when he gave her a ceramic bear holding a purple heart, with a place for a tea-candle. He told her it was because he appreciated seeing the heart light and hoped she would continue to bring it to all of the concerts.

Driving ninety miles an hour home one minute and fifty the next, the girls giggled and sang and appreciated every moment of their good fortune spent following the boys. Another amazing concert attended, followed by yet more surprises from their favorite band members.

Madison teased Allison all the way home, saying Donovan had it bad for her, and that she wasn't as giddy about him as he was for her. "It's like you're the star, and he's your biggest fan. I swear he has it bad." Madison repeated herself several times, with several different examples.

But Allison denied it all. "What would a major pop star want with the likes of an ordinary, boring, nothing, like me from Daytona Beach?" Madison could try all she wanted, but she would never convince Allison that Donovan was anything but grateful for all of the attention. "And besides, what would I want with a rich, good-looking, pop star who's gone all of the time, when I have... Trenton." Allison laughed.

Chapter Two

The girls knew it would be almost a month before seeing the band again. Dillonsledge would be traveling through the Carolinas, Jersey, and New York. They would make their way over to Detroit and down through Ohio, Kentucky and Tennessee before getting back to Atlanta. Then, they'd work their way across the states, ending in California. The only time the girls regretted living in Florida was when the boys were on tour. Their number of concerts was limited because of their limited amount of time off work, and how far they had to go. (Limited at least in their opinions, but everyone else couldn't believe they went to so many concerts!)

The upcoming concert in Atlanta was happening only because Donovan sent them tickets, and then begged Allison's manager on the phone one day to let her off from work so she could go. Being a fan himself, and ecstatic at the thought of talking to an actual star, Mr. Gillespie graciously arranged the schedule to make sure she had several days off that weekend.

Allison couldn't wait to get back to work after this last concert and tell everyone what happened. They always gave her a hard time being such a devoted fan, and going to see the same concert so many times. So every time something different happened, she just had to share all of the details. She giggled as she parked the car, knowing there were several details she would have to leave out this time.

Allison made her way into Shiley's, the biggest department store in the mall. She loved working at the mall. She got to meet so many people. She loved Shiley's too. It was the only place she had ever worked. She started working between her junior and senior years of high school part-time after school. She definitely worked her way up in the company, starting at the very bottom. She continued to work part-time until her second year of college. At that point, she started working full-time and going to school part-time. It took longer for her to get her degree, but when the women's department manager position became available, she couldn't pass on the chance for advancement. Shortly after she received her Bachelor's degrees in Business Administration and Business Management, the assistant store manager retired and Allison was offered that position. Betty said she had worked an extra year, waiting for Allison to finish school so she could take the position. Mr. Gillespie had been instrumental in getting Betty to stay, begging her for just one more year, so he could give the position to Allison.

Allison smirked as she passed so many people on their way to work who couldn't smile that early in the morning. She didn't know if it was because they weren't awake yet, or because they hated their jobs. And she couldn't help but smile and say good morning to every one of them, quietly laughing to herself for being so evil.

"Good morning, Trenton." Allison wondered just how much she should tell him.

"Hello, my love! So do tell, am I going to have to play knight and rescue the woman I love from the awful grips of that dragon, Donovan?" Trenton teased her as much or more about the band than anyone else did.

"You won't believe what happened this time!"

Trenton rolled his eyes. "I'm not sure anything would surprise me anymore! But if he asked you to marry him, I hope you told him no."

Allison thought for a second that she shouldn't tell him because he had such a crush on her, but she was bursting at the seams, ready to tell the first person she saw, and it just happened to be him. She decided to tell him they got to go to the hotel this time, but left spending the night for the next person. She didn't think rubbing the sex in Trenton's face would be very nice, since she had continuously denied his advances.

Allison liked Trenton Stewart, a fellow co-worker, and a complete nerd. He was a nice guy, and a hard worker. Trenton has had a crush on her since their first meeting and has managed to remind her every day since. They are just friends, good friends, and the crush eventually turned into something of a joke between them. Unlike Allison, Shiley's was a part-time gig for Trenton. He was moving on to bigger and better things in the computer industry. He usually worked in the evening, but came in early once and a while when he was out of class. He helped in the stock room most of the time, but often offered much needed assistance in the office, designing new programs to help the managers.

Before work started, Mr. Gillespie had a meeting. He

wanted to let everyone know that overtime hours were available. Tom, their coworker from men's wear, had been mugged in the parking lot and beaten up badly. He was doing better, but would have to stay in the hospital for a few days. Before he closed the meeting, he reminded everyone to buddy-up before leaving.

Throughout the day, Allison only spoke about Donovan to a few other interested coworkers, but never told Trenton the rest of the story. That afternoon, Madison called Allison to see how Trenton took the news and asked if she was going to have lunch in her office or go down to the food court.

Madison worked a few stores down from Shiley's at Just Shoes, in the office doing bookkeeping and scheduling for the company's local stores. They almost always had lunch together, and they usually ate down in the food court. Today was no different. "Trenton's not going to get mad because you won't even go out with him, but you slept with Donovan, is he?" Madison knew Trenton really liked Allison, and even though they were good friends, he wanted more.

"No! Trenton is harmless. He knows I see other guys. He never said anything about them."

"Okay! Good. So how did everyone take the latest news flash?"

Allison laughed. "Some refused to believe it, but others wanted more details than I was willing to give. How 'bout you?"

"Same story! Has Donovan called you yet today?" Allison showed Madison where he had called three times already since they got home.

"Oh, guess what?" Allison paused momentarily and waited for Madison to say 'what'? "Do you remember that guy Tom, from work, the one I got all those sizes from last week? I met him in the parking lot after work by his truck. He got the crap beat out of him in the parking lot after work one night. They said it was a mugging. He is still in the hospital."

Madison sat there with her mouth open, in shock. "I don't know what to say. Our mall? Someone we know! You were just with him. We are going to buy clothes for his kids!"

"I know! I know!" Allison felt the same way. After lunch they parted ways and went back to work.

Trenton was pouting when Allison walked in. She tried to talk to him, but he would have nothing to do with her. He finally told her he was disappointed in her for not telling him the whole story, and then left work early.

Allison hated that she had hurt him by not telling him, but she thought she was protecting him. She would try to explain it to him the next time she saw him. She went about her business, not letting the way Trenton felt affect her work. She managed to get the timecards done and design the layout for the upcoming ad before it was time to go home. She left instructions for the evening staff, letting them know what needed to be done, and clocked out.

That night Madison's brother, Mason, was having a party at his house, and Madison and Allison were invited. Madison picked Allison up at seven-thirty. They were asked to stop and get the wings and pizzas Mason ordered. By the time they arrived, Mason's friend, Taylor, was already there, and he had already started drinking. He immediately started hitting on Madison, asking if she was going to go all the way with him before the night was over. Mason gave him a big shove and told him Madi and Alli were off limits, that he needed to leave them alone.

Taylor immediately backed off, for the most part, and gave them a half-hearted apology. As guests arrived, things quickly got out of control. When Taylor made drunken advances towards her, Allison told Madison she would be waiting outside, away from all of the nonsense, until she was ready to go. Allison sat out back on the swing, enjoying the music she could hear coming from inside. She heard the back door open, and saw Taylor coming outside. She tried to sneak around the tree beside the swing and get around to the side of the house before he saw her. She planned to go around the house and back through the front door without being noticed.

Allison stopped at the corner of the house, to look back and see if he was following her. He spun her around, pushing her up against the side of the house, kissing her hard on the mouth, and feeling under her shirt. Allison tried to scream, but he put his hand over her mouth. She kicked and struggled as an instant reaction. She finally calmed down enough to gather her wits and think of where his hands and legs were, so she could actually defend herself instead of just wearing herself out. She managed to connect a solid punch to the side of his head. It all happened so fast. He kicked her legs out from under her, throwing her to the ground. She bit one of his fingers covering her mouth and kicked him in the groin, throwing him off to the side on impact. She tried to run, but he grabbed her leg. She kicked him in the head several times with her other foot, and pulled away, rushing into the house.

Allison finally settled down and told Madison what had

happened. Madison told Mason right away, and they all went outside to see where Taylor was. He was already gone. Mason said it was just as well, or he would have kicked his ass! "Do you want me to call the police, Allison?" Mason felt really bad; Allison was like a sister to him.

Allison was still a basket of nerves, and pretty shaken up. "I don't know. Is he like this all of the time?"

"No! If he was like that all of the time, I wouldn't be friends with him! I have never seen him like this. He must have been doing drugs or something." Mason wasn't trying to make excuses for him, and wanted him to pay for what he had done.

"He's gone. Let's just forget about it. We don't need to call the police." Allison wanted the whole ordeal out of her mind as quickly as possible.

"Well, I'm not going to forget about it any time soon. You can bet the next time I see him, I am going to say something! And after tonight, he is no longer welcome around me or any of my family and friends!" Mason promised, and then sent everyone home.

Allison turned all the lights on in her little apartment after Madison dropped her off. She looked in all the closets, behind all of the doors, and under the bed. After a long, hot shower, she curled up on the couch and finally dozed off, with the TV and all of the lights still on. She jumped, and fell off of the couch when someone knocked on her front door. She crawled over to the door, like she was trying to keep them from seeing her. She was getting ready to look out the peep hole when the person on the other side of the door knocked again, introducing himself.

"Ms. Drexler? I am Detective Drake Larson. I need to check on you and ask you some questions about your altercation earlier this evening."

Allison slowly stood up, finally looking out the peep hole. She asked the detective to step down to the window by the kitchen, and asked to see his badge, and his driver's license. The detective giggled, reaching into his back pocket to get his wallet.

Allison thanked him and told him she would be right back. She looked out the window again after she grabbed her robe, and then slowly opened the door. "I told Mason not to call the police. He said Taylor was not usually like that."

"Yes ma'am. Mason did not call the police. But we did talk with Mason and his sister, Madison, earlier. Ms. Cannon said she dropped you off here around ten o'clock. Is that correct, ma'am?"

"Oh my God! Did something happen to Madison?" Allison got really upset.

"No ma'am, Ms. Cannon's fine. What time did she drop you off?"

"Ten. If Madison is fine, and Mason didn't call the police, then what are you doing here at…" Allison looked around to see the clock.

"It's two o'clock ma'am. Did you leave and go anywhere after Ms. Cannon dropped you off?"

"No. I turned every light on, looked in all the closets and got a long, hot shower. I guess I was more upset than I thought, and still a little scared from earlier."

"That stands to reason, ma'am. About earlier, can you tell me what happened?" Allison told Detective Larson everything she could remember, starting with picking the wings and pizza up, about Mason telling Taylor they were off limits, to going back outside only to find out Taylor had already left. She left nothing out. "Thank you, Ms. Drexler. I am sorry you had to go through that. But I can promise you, you don't have to worry about Mr. Landon again. He won't be able to hurt you anymore."

Allison's knees became weak. Detective Larson reached out to hold her up. "Are you all right, ma'am?" He helped her to a kitchen chair where he told her to sit down.

"Are you telling me something happened to Taylor tonight... after he left the party?"

"Yes Ms. Drexler. We received a call around twelve o'clock. Some kids found Mr. Landon's body in an empty lot, down by the pier. He had been beaten up pretty badly and died from a strong blow to the head. I'm sorry to have to put you through this so late at night, but we are trying to figure out what happened." The detective was very apologetic.

"That's okay officer, I understand. I'll be happy to help in any way I can. Unfortunately, I don't know very much."

"That's okay, ma'am. Thank you for your time. If I can just get you to fill this out for me, I'll let you get back to sleep. I will call you if I need more information. And this is my card, with my direct number, in case you think of something else. Good night, Ms. Drexler."

Chapter Three

———— ✎ ————

Allison could not sleep. She kept replaying the Taylor incident over and over in her head. All she could picture was the way she got away...'a strong blow' to his head with her fist, before he threw her to the ground. Allison kept hearing the officer's words repeated in her mind, 'beaten up, and died from a strong blow to his head.' Allison had kicked him in the head when he grabbed her other leg. She felt the sudden urge to puke and rushed to the bathroom. She lay on the bathroom floor, crying, thinking she was the one who had killed Taylor. Allison stripped and sat in the shower with the cool water running down over her.

Madison couldn't sleep either, and was worried about her friend. She knew how Allison's mind worked, and knew somehow she would be blaming herself. She tried calling Allison several times, but got no answer. She even left messages, urging Allison to call her back immediately.

Madison called Mason. "I have got to go over there. You know how she thinks. She is blaming herself right now for his death somehow. And she is not answering the phone. I am really worried about her. I have got to go Mason!"

"Okay. Well, you are a big girl. I'm not going to tell

you 'You can't'. But be careful. And call me if you need anything. Do you want me to meet you there?"

"No. I will be fine. But thanks for always having my back bro. Love you."

Allison was still in the shower when Madison got there. Madison freaked out when Allison did not answer the door. She hated to use her key, since it was only for emergencies, but at the moment, this was a very big emergency. She unlocked the door, opening it slowly, calling Allison's name. Allison's silence scared Madison even more. Madison finally heard the shower. She called Allison's name again, louder this time when she got to the room so Allison could hear her over the water. Allison screamed!

Madison did not care that there was puke everywhere, or that Allison was naked, wet, and the shower was still running; she was just glad to see that Allison was all right. She opened the shower door, crying tears of joy, and hugged Allison. "I was so worried about you!"

Allison started bawling. "I killed Taylor!" Madison kicked her shoes off, adjusted the temperature of the water to make it warmer, and sat on the other side of the shower, holding Allison's hands. She was certain Allison did not really kill anyone, but at that moment, it was going to take a lot to convince Allison of that. Madison started off by telling Allison it wasn't her fault. And that under no circumstances would she ever kill anybody, no matter what they had done to her.

However, Allison had thoroughly convinced herself it was her swift hit to the side of his head that caused the damage that killed Taylor. And that she only made it worse when she kicked him in the same spot just seconds later. Madison almost laughed at her delicate friend's conviction. She had to be tactful in letting her friend know that she was not that strong. It would take more than a fist from her to kill someone. And although the kick might have put him in a daze, it wouldn't be enough to kill him either.

Madison carefully searched for just the right words to help her friend see the light. "I think we need to call Detective Larson. If you killed Taylor, we need to let him know it was in self defense." Okay, so Madison took the easy way out, and decided it best to recruit some help. "Even though I think it probably took a whole lot more than what you dished out to kill him."

Allison stood up. She was still in shock and moving slowly. Madison grabbed the towel, wrapped it around Allison, and then reached into the closet to get one for her. "Let's get you dressed and me changed, call Detective Larson, and get this matter cleared up!"

Detective Larson was still out in the field, but agreed to come by and talk with Allison after Madison told him what she was thinking. While the girls waited, Madison cleaned the bathroom floor and went over the details with Allison, trying to convince her friend that she didn't have anything to do with the death of Taylor.

When the detective arrived, he was very supportive while listening to Allison's confession. "Ms. Drexler, I appreciate your willingness to help with this matter. But I have to tell you, I've seen Mr. Landon's body, and ma'am, not to question your strength, especially in a fight or flight situation, but I am more than certain that the defense you inflicted on Mr. Landon was not the cause of his death."

"But I hit him on the head, and then kicked him in the same place. You said he died from a blow to the head. I didn't mean to hurt him. I was just trying to get away." Allison sobbed and was still not convinced.

"Ma'am, I'm not supposed to discuss the details of an ongoing investigation, but under the circumstances, I have to let you know... Mr. Landon was murdered. He was beaten to death. His body shows evidence of multiple wounds, and a skull fracture caused by a blunt object. I know for a fact that if you had caused that kind of damage to Mr. Landon, we wouldn't have found him in that empty lot, but beside the house instead. Rest assured Ms. Drexler, you did not kill anyone here tonight."

For the first time in several hours, Allison took a nice long relaxing breath. Allison kind of giggled, then started bawling again, gasping for air, trying to talk. "I... thought... I... killed him!"

Detective Larson hugged her, wiping her tears. "Shh. You probably didn't even hurt him. But next time, go towards the crowd, instead of away from it. I understand you were trying to hide, but there were a lot of people inside. If you have a choice and there are people close by, don't try to hide by yourself. That goes for you too, Ms. Cannon. Okay!"

Allison nodded. Madison thanked the detective for coming by when he had so much work to do and showed him to the door. Madison said she was staying the rest of the night. "It's already four o'clock. We need to call and let them know we won't be coming into work today."

"I know. I am so tired!"

Madison laughed. "Well killing people takes a lot out of you." She could not resist.

Allison threw a pillow at her. "Oh, shut up!" Allison laughed, and then got serious. "I was scared. I really thought I hurt him by kicking him and that he died because of it." There was a short moment of silence. "I can't believe Taylor is dead. One minute he was right there, and the next he's down by the pier, murdered. What if the murderer was at Mason's house, and would have gotten me, if Taylor hadn't come outside when he did?"

"Don't even think about that! No what-ifs allowed! Understand?" Madison was not about to let her friend go to the endless number of possibilities. "You didn't have anything to do with it, and that's all you need to know. So... since we're not going to work, do you want to watch some boys?" They both called their managers at home, explaining what happened and let them know they would not be able to make it into work. Then they popped some popcorn and got out the tape of the Dillonsledge concert from the year before.

Madison was glad to know Allison was doing much better. They laughed and sang to the tape, watching as much as they could before fatigue took over and they had to go to sleep. From the couch, Madison could hear Allison in the bedroom crying. She got up, climbed into bed with Allison, wiping her tears. "Shh. Everything is going to be fine. Detective Larson will find out what really happened. Now quit thinking so much and try to go to sleep. I am here! And I won't let anything happen to you." Madison reached over, using the remote to see if Allison had any music in the CD player. Dillonsledge started playing, as she suspected. She turned the volume down and curled up, holding Allison in her arms like a little child.

The following afternoon, Madison and Allison dressed and went to the mall. They wanted to let everyone know they were okay and see if there was anything they needed to do. Allison was getting ready to leave the store when she passed Trenton, who was just coming in to work. He grabbed her by the arm, pulling her over to the corner and told her he really needed to talk to her.

Allison noticed a small cut on his face. "Trenton, what happened to you?"

"I kind of got into a little fight. I followed you to that party last night and…"

"You what?" Allison was furious. "How dare you?" She pulled away from the grasp he still had on her arm.

"Wait, let me explain." Trenton grabbed her shoulders with both hands, turning her around to face him. "I was upset yesterday when you didn't trust me enough to tell me the truth. I had to hear it from one of the other guys. I had no right to talk to you the way I did, and I wanted to apologize. I came by your apartment to talk to you, but Madison had just pulled out of the drive. I followed you. I know it was wrong, that is why I didn't approach you. I didn't want to look like some pathetic stalker. I promise you I am not!" He let his hands slide down her arms, trying to hold her hands.

Allison shook her head, and pulled her hands back. "Trent, I didn't want to hurt your feelings. That's why I didn't say anything to you about sleeping with Donovan. I didn't think you wanted to hear anything like that."

"You're right. I did not want to hear it, but it did happen, and since it happened, I wanted to hear it from you. We are supposed to be friends Alli."

"We are friends, just friends and nothing more. You know that. But if you're going to get all defensive or possessive, then we won't even be able to be friends." Allison was the one who was disappointed now. She turned to go.

"Allison, wait." Trenton reached for her arm again, with no success. "I left the party, knowing I couldn't talk to you there, but I was so upset with myself for talking to you that way, I came back. I had to see you, to apologize!" He looked around to make sure no one was close. He took a step closer to Allison. "I saw that guy attack you, Allison. By the time I parked the car and called out for you, you had already made it back into the house. I approached the guy, but he hit me and took off, that's where I got the scratch on my face."

"Why didn't you let us know you were there?" Trenton put his head down. "I didn't want you to think I was stalking you. So, I left as soon as I knew that guy was gone and that you were safe."

"If you didn't want me to know then, why are you telling me now?"

"I'm only saying something now, because of the picture in the paper this morning. I think the guy in the paper is the guy that hit me last night." He reached into his pocket and pulled out a crumpled piece of newspaper, showing her the picture.

"It is him, Trenton! We need to call Detective Larson and let him know you were there." Allison fumbled through her handbag looking for the detective's card.

"No! I can't let you do that. Why do you want to call him? I told you I left, and I don't know anything to tell him."

"Calm down Trenton! We have to let him know you were there, and that he hit you. What if he has your DNA under his fingernails or something? You don't want them to think you are hiding something do you?"

"No! But I don't want them to think I was retaliating on your behalf and that I did something stupid, like kill him or anything either. Because I did not!"

"That's good to know. I did not either. Are you going to let me call Larson or not?"

"Okay." Trenton reluctantly agreed.

Madison finished at Just Shoes and met Allison in her office, as planned. She was surprised to see Detective Larson there. Allison told her what Trenton had said, as they watched him give his statement. Detective Larson walked the girls out to their car when he finished with Trenton.

"You did the right thing by calling Ms. Drexler. I'm glad to see you're doing better. How did you sleep?"

Madison answered for her, because she knew Allison would skirt around the truth, not totally lying, but not being completely honest either. "She tossed and turned and had bad dreams all night."

"Well, she's lucky to have such a good friend to take care of her. I'm glad you were able to stay with her last night. She didn't need to be alone."

He turned to Allison. "As for you, I work nights, so you can call me any time. If you wake up having a bad dream and cannot go back to sleep, or if you ever feel uncomfortable, or scared I can come by and check your apartment for you. No one should ever feel scared in their own home. Okay. You have my number. Use it if you need to."

Chapter Four

Dillonsledge was on their way to Atlanta. Donovan called Allison to see when they were going to be there. "We just left the concert in Nashville and we're on our way to Atlanta. What time do you think you'll be there tomorrow?"

"We plan on leaving in the morning and driving up." Allison's voice was groggy because Donovan woke her up. "It takes around six hours to get there from here. So we'll probably be there around four o'clock."

"Okay. I was kind of hoping you could be there a little earlier."

"We worked all day today. We thought it would be better to sleep all night and then drive tomorrow, so we didn't have to pay for another night at a hotel."

"That's okay, maybe we can have dinner instead of lunch. Is that all right?"

"That sounds fine. I'm going to let you go though, so I can go back to sleep."

"Okay Allison. Good night. Call me when you get to Atlanta tomorrow so I can let you know where to go."

"We can get our own hotel Donovan. You don't have to pay for it. You already gave us the tickets."

"I know, but I have ulterior motives, that we'll talk about more tomorrow."

"Good night, Donovan. See you sometime tomorrow." Allison's alarm went off at seven-thirty. She stayed in bed, staring into the ceiling, thinking about what Donovan had said about his ulterior motives. She felt cheap, and used, wondering how many other 'playthings' Donovan had. Her only consolation was the fact that they had been talking on the phone for almost two years now; and he still calls her more than she calls him. She finished rummaging through her things to make sure she hadn't forgotten something. She packed her lacy teddy as a surprise for Donovan, knowing that most of his flings weren't planned in advance, so at least this would be something different.

After checking to make sure everything was turned off, and/or unplugged, Allison packed the car and called Madison to let her know she was on the way over an hour ahead of schedule.

Madison was ready and waiting when she got there. "I should have called you at six, when I got up."

"Hum, no. You should have turned over and went back to sleep. You're going to be so tired tonight now."

"I'm sure Derek will be able to keep me awake."

"Oh, really?"

"Yep. He called me to make sure I knew I was staying with him tonight, in a totally separate room, not just the other room… wait… that didn't come out right. At any rate, we'll have a separate room all to ourselves this time."

"I'm kind of disappointed. This is the first time I'm not that excited about going to hear the boys in concert."

"I'm extremely excited, and ready to hear Derek sing again. Boy can that boy make some music!"

"I'm glad we'll have our own rooms tonight. He made you sing a little loud last time."

"And I was even holding back. But Donovan wasn't that quiet either."

"I know. I told him to shut up or get off."

"Oh, he was getting off all right!"

"Madison!"

"What?"

Allison turned the music up and started singing. The drive to Atlanta wasn't that bad, once they got there however it was usual congestion. It was always bad going through downtown Atlanta, unless it was the wee-hours- of-the-morning. Allison got her phone out and told Madison to call Donovan, so she could concentrate on driving. Madison told her where the boys were staying and how to get there. Donovan was watching out the window when they pulled up. He dialed Allison's number to let her know he could see her. She turned around and waved, blowing him a kiss.

Some young girls in the parking lot saw what she was doing and looked up to see Donovan. He threw the curtain back and started waving to everyone. Of course the girls all rushed over to their car, asking questions, and wanting to know if she was Donovan's girlfriend. Allison assured them she was not, and that they were just friends.

A bodyguard Donovan had sent to rescue them stepped between the crowd and Allison and Madison. He led them all the way up to their rooms. Donovan and Derek were standing in the doorways waiting. Derek rushed out to take Madison's bag, so Donovan followed suit.

Allison took Madison's hand, pulling her back for a hug. "I guess I'll see you at the concert, if I don't see you before."

"No offense, but I hope I don't have a chance to see you before the concert." Madison raised her eyebrows up and down.

Allison was greeted by a big hug from Donovan, and an exceptionally long, passionate kiss. "I missed you!" Donovan led her to the couch. He sat down and pulled her down onto his lap, gently pushing the hair out of her face. "As soon as this tour is over, I want us to go away together."

Allison was blindsided, and speechless. Donovan saw the surprise in her eyes. "I'll need a long vacation after the tour is over, and I can't think of anyone I'd rather have with me. You don't have to answer now; I just want you to think about it."

"Wow! I will have to plan strategically, but I might be able to finagle a few weeks off together. I should have plenty of vacation time, since the only time I take off is a day or two here and there to come see you."

"I like that you come to see me. When am I going to get an invite to come and see you for a change?" Donovan was full of ideas that knocked her socks off. Allison did not have time to respond. Donovan scooped her up and sat her down on the couch beside him, swinging her leg to the outside of his body as he rolled over on top of her.

He braced himself, looking into her eyes for approval. "We have a couple of hours before dinner…" Allison rubbed his strong arms, the muscles flexed as he held himself up. She rose to kiss him, her body reacting immediately. She stopped him, asking if he had protection. He nodded, taking her in his arms, carrying her to the bedroom.

29

Allison didn't worry about vacationing after the tour, or inviting him to stay with her. She concentrated on the here and now, memorizing every muscle, every moan. This boy was well practiced, and she intended to take full advantage of everything he had to offer. They finally showered and dressed for dinner. Donovan called Derek and the other boys to see if they were ready to leave. Madison blushed when she came out of Derek's room, knowing everyone knew what they had been doing.

Derek reminded everyone who Madison was, by name only. Donovan introduced Allison as his girlfriend, which caught everyone off guard, including her. Dillon had his wife, Natalie. And Dominic had his wife, Leslie. The bodyguards escorted them to the limo and said they would see them at the restaurant. During dinner, Dillon told the girls about his built-on studio and about how the band got its name. The boys were all neighbors growing up. Dillon started playing guitar at an early age and used to sit on his bedroom window seal, with his legs hanging outside. That is how he taught himself to play without watching where his fingers went.

Derek took lessons and started playing the piano when he heard Dillon play the guitar the first time. He was impressed and wanted to play the guitar at first but found he could play the piano much better. Donovan felt left out when they would get together to play, because all Dillon and Derek wanted to do was play music. So Dillon gave him a guitar and told him to start playing, as a joke. Donovan signed up to take bass lessons, surprising them two weeks later by playing with them. Dominic was the last to join. He told them he could not play the guitar or the piano. Dillon wanted him to play the saxophone, he had always liked the way it sounded. Dominic tried, but didn't have any luck with that either. One day Derek brought his brother's play drum set over and told Dominic to try them on for size. They were impressed by how well he held the beat.

The only thing they needed after that was a name. Dillon's parents added on to Dillon's room the first year the boys started playing music together, to give them a place to practice. They cut the wall out where the window used to be and added on to that side of the house. Because they had teased Dillon about sitting on his window ledge all of the time, and the ledge was no longer there, the new room ended up being called Dillon's Ledge. Derek's parents bought the boys a neon sign with the name of the room on it when the room was finished. The boys liked the name and kept it as the name of their band, but made it one word because it looked better, and would give everyone something to talk about.

Allison and Madison had already heard the story, but enjoyed hearing it from the boys themselves. Donovan leaned over and finally told her they would be sitting up front with the wives during the concert. Allison protested, saying he had spent so much money on the tickets it would be a shame not to use them. Donovan just shook his head. She had no idea how the business worked, but that was part of what attracted him to her. After dinner, they all went back to the hotel to rest for a while before the concert started. Donovan and Allison decided to take a nap, unlike Derek and Madison.

Derek called later and told them to stop whatever they were doing, because it was time to go to the venue. Donovan asked for their tickets. When they got to the stadium, he told the boys they needed to do a little PR work and give away a couple of really good seats. Donovan had Allison and Madison go out into the crowd and find someone that wasn't able to get tickets for the concert. The girls loved the idea, and said they would do it, as long as they could bring them in with them, so they could sit through the sound check, and go backstage before the concert. It was way more than what Donovan had in mind, but after discussing it with the other band members, they agreed.

Allison and Madison made their way through the crowds of people. Near the back of the crowd, they saw a scalper trying to sell tickets. They watched as a young woman with her son approached the scalpers to see how much they wanted for the tickets. The woman shook her head, and the boy started to cry again. Allison and Madison knew they had found their winners. Allison and Madison were almost in tears themselves as they walked up to the woman. It was obvious the woman couldn't afford concert tickets, but was trying her luck, in hopes of catching a break for her son.

Allison whispered in the young woman's ear, as Madison bent down to make friends with the boy. "Hi. My name is Allison Drexler. We are here representing the boys, because they couldn't come out into the crowd. They sent us out here to give away two really good seats to the concert tonight. You don't have tickets already, do you?"

The woman's face lit up. "No. Is this for real... because it's not a very funny joke?"

Allison smiled. "This is very real. And Madison and I told them we would only do this for them if they would let us take you backstage right now to meet them and let you sit in on the sound check."

"And you picked us?" The young woman started crying, hugging her son.

"Yes. Are you ready to meet the band?" The woman did not tell her son where they were going, so he was completely surprised when Madison flipped the curtain back and they were actually on stage. The bigger his eyes got, the higher he jumped, the louder he squealed. His mother just cried. She thanked the band many times, for giving her son something she would never have been able to. And she hugged Allison and Madison telling them she would never forget them, or what they had done for her and her son.

Dillon let the boy hold his guitar, and showed him how to strum the strings. Dominic lured him away with the drum sticks, until Derek gave him a microphone and asked him if he knew any of the words. They let him sing along, while they did the sound check. From the way the young boy acted, it was by far the best thing that had ever happened to him. As for all of the boys, truth be known, they decided they needed to do things like that more often.

Chapter Five

Dillonsledge was a popular band, loved by their fans, and known to many as a giving group. Things like giving away tickets, letting fans attend the sound checks, signing autographs and taking pictures were all things that got attention from the press. Very few negative things had ever been said in the magazines or papers about the band Dillonsledge, or its members.

Donovan hugged Allison. "You did a good thing. She couldn't afford even the cheapest tickets, now look at them." The young boy was dancing with Derek, trying to learn the dance moves. Allison was proud of what they had just done, knowing this was something the young boy would never forget. He was grinning from ear to ear, laughing, and having the time of his life. The boys gave him a microphone of his own during sound check, so he could sing along. Of course it wasn't turned on, and no one could hear him, but he didn't know that.

The young mother hung out with the girls, while her son tagged along with the boys as they got ready for the concert. Just before the show started, everyone met backstage for a pep talk. Dillon thanked everyone for being a part of the show and for all of their hard work. The body guard showed the mother and son to their seats, while Allison and Madison made their way down front with the wives. During the show, Donovan kept stopping in front of Allison, making gestures and blowing her kisses. It was different watching the show from that close, not like watching the whole production from a distance. Allison spent a lot of the time concentrating on Donovan, and missed most of the other things going on, so she wasn't so sure that she actually liked being that close.

Before they started the last song, Dillon introduced the mother and son as their special guests, and had one of the body guards escort them up on stage. Dillon presented the boy with one of his acoustic guitars, signed by all of the band members. Everyone was crying, including the band members. It was by far the best show ever. Allison ran up and hugged Dillon after the concert, thanking him for doing such a grand gesture.

"Hey! Save some of that for me." Donovan teased.

"Oh, don't worry, you'll get yours later!" Allison let him know there was plenty where that came from and he would be getting it, and a whole lot more, in just a little bit. And did he ever, Allison was so hyped after the concert. She was always excited, but tonight, she had gotten a taste of what it was like to be a small part of it. She couldn't imagine how the boys must feel after a concert. The endorphins took over and she didn't even let Donovan finish his shower by himself; she couldn't wait any longer; so much for the surprise teddy.

"Every night can be just like this, you and me, city after city. What do you say?"

Allison was completely surprised. She pulled the sheet

up, turning to face him. But she did not know what to say. "You don't want me with you, all of the time. It will be different, than just talking on the phone once and a while, or having really good sex now and then after a few of the concerts. It will be different."

"It would be different. But that's not to say it still wouldn't be okay." Donovan snuggled up against her. "And don't tell me I don't want you! You have no idea how much I want you." Allison closed her eyes and dozed off; dreaming of what it might be like to have a relationship with Donovan. She had never thought about it before, because there was no chance of it ever happening. But now, it was a possibility! And not only was it a possibility, but whether or not it happened… was completely up to her.

The following morning, Donovan called Derek to see if he and Madison wanted to join them for breakfast before the band had to leave for Texas. Derek and Madison were already downstairs in the dining room. They were lovey-dovey, and seemed to be getting along very well. Madison picked over her breakfast, as did Derek. Donovan picked over his breakfast also. Allison on the other hand, had quite an appetite, and even ate one of Madison's pancakes. Saying goodbye took longer than usual for Derek and Madison, but Allison kissed Donovan on the cheek and told him to call when he got to Texas. She did not give him a chance to get mushy, or sentimental.

Madison was almost in tears when she finally got to the car. This was their last concert for this tour. They wouldn't see the boys in concert again until the next album came out. "I can't believe this tour is already over for us. We need to try and fly out to see the boys at one of the concerts in

California, or maybe in Vegas." Madison was ready to follow them to Texas.

"I know! You and Derek were really quiet at breakfast, and neither one of you hardly ate a thing. Something happened; bad, or really, really good? I hope good!"

Madison blushed and started crying. "I never should have slept with him. I knew I wouldn't be able to just walk away. I want more, and I'm never going to have it."

Allison felt so bad. Donovan wanted more too, and she didn't know if she'd be able to give it to him. She decided not to say anything about it to Madison. "We always said we'd be grateful for anything we got. We have gotten so much. You have to get over the initial shock that it happened. You will be fine. It is only natural to want more. We all do. And we just have to realize we have so much more than most fans ever get. That will be our strength."

They spent the ride home the same way they spent every ride home after a concert. Allison could not keep quiet about Donovan any longer once she saw Madison had finally calmed down. "I think you were right about Donovan after all."

"About what?"

"Remember when you said he was giddier than I was? I'm not sure if he is serious, or if he was just pillow-talking, but he said every night could be like that."

"Oh my God! What did you say?" Madison was in shock. "And why didn't you tell me earlier?"

"I was trying to remember everything he said and figure out if he really meant it or not."

"Well, what do you think?" Madison loved her friend, but at that moment, she wished she could be in that dilemma.

"I'm not sure, I guess only time will tell. He already asked when I was going to invite him to come to see me for a change. And told me not to tell him he didn't want me, that I had no idea how much he wanted me." Allison could see the desire in Madison's eyes. "So do you think you could give everything you've worked for away, just to go with Derek on the road?"

"For a sure thing? Yes, I think I could! If we were in a committed relationship and things were working out okay. I would at least consider it. For a possibility, giving everything away, and not having anything to come back to if we broke up? That's not a chance I'd be willing to take."

"That's all I've been thinking about since he said that. I am not sure that I could give it all up, even if we were married. He would be gone so much. I love what he does. Boy, do I love what he does, musically speaking... well everything else too, but musically speaking. I love their music, the concerts, and I would support him in anything he wanted to do, or anywhere he wanted to go. But, I don't think I could quit everything I do and love just to follow him everywhere."

"I know what you mean. I want more. I am not going to deny it. This morning if Derek had asked me to leave everything and go with him, I would have told you that I loved you, and that I would call, and then I would have gotten on the bus with him. But you are right. We can't put our own lives aside and forget about them, just to be with someone we don't really know, unless we know it's going to be forever. Although, during the next tour, I wouldn't mind trying to schedule two weeks off during the concerts to travel with them. That would be so cool."

"We might actually be able to do that! If they still like us by then?" The girls cut up, laughing, and having a good time on the way back home. Home, somewhere they both felt comfortable, with their families close, and good jobs; all things they knew they'd never be able to leave behind, not even for Dillonsledge.

Monday morning, it was back to work as usual, sharing stories of the last concert and all of the excitement. Allison gave Mr. Gillespie an autographed picture of the band, for letting her have Thursday and Friday off. He thanked her and told her that was okay, because he was taking Monday and Tuesday off next week. Allison promised herself she would tell Trenton everything this time, whether he wanted to hear it or not.

"Welcome back. I didn't think I'd see you until tomorrow." Trenton put his things in his locker and followed Allison back to her office.

"I needed to double check everyone's time before I sent the final copy through to the office. And I wanted to talk to the evening shift to see if there was any trouble over the weekend. And talk to you."

"To me?" Trenton was curious. "About what?"

"Well, I didn't want the same thing to happen this time as it did after the last concert. I wanted to tell you what happened, so you did not hear it from anyone else, since we are friends. Are you prepared to hear all of it?"

"All of it? That must mean you're going to tell me something I don't really want to hear."

"It's not much different than the last time, except this

time, he told me every night could be like it was that night. And what a night it was!"

"So, he wants to see more of you? What did you tell him?" He knew what she told him would not make a difference in their relationship, but he still wanted to know.

"He also asked me when I was going to invite him here, to see me for a change. I didn't give him a real answer. I just told him he didn't really want me. Of course, he quickly let me know I shouldn't say that, because I didn't have a clue how much he wanted me."

"Wow! It sounds like he really likes you and wants to get to know you. You should let him come here to see you. What could it hurt? Unless there is some small chance you really want me instead." Trenton held his hands up like he was praying.

Allison pushed his hands back down and started to say something, but Trenton said it instead. "I know, just friends."

She hugged him. "Yes, but a very good friend." Trenton went to work, going through stock that had been delivered and separating it into the different departments. Allison made her way to the floor to talk with the staff and the department managers.

Chapter Six

There were already several things in Allison's life that she often regretted, not going to Greece during her sophomore year of college with her boyfriend at the time and another couple, passing on the opportunity to speak at her graduation when the speech she wrote was better than the one she had to listen to, and not going down to the pier the day Paramount was signing up extras for the movie that was being filmed there. She didn't want anything else to be added to that list. It had been over a week since the concert in Atlanta, and Donovan continued to remind her about the vacation after the tour.

She liked Donovan very much. She couldn't figure out why she was so hesitant to say yes to the idea of going on an all expenses paid vacation with someone she obviously had a good time with. She flashed back in her mind to the pictures she saw of the Greece vacation she neglected to take. "Error on the side of caution…" kept running through her mind. If she said yes, and hurt him, at least she got to go on a nice vacation. She could easily go for a free vacation, and not have to see him again unless she really wanted to. But she liked Donovan too much to use him like that. People used him all the time. Part of why he liked her so much was because she was different.

Allison finished the laundry and loaded the car. She hated going to the laundry mat, but at least during this time of day there were not many people there and it didn't take her very long.

"What's a nice girl like you doing in a place like this?"

Allison's heart stopped. She quickly checked out her surroundings, turning to see who belonged to the somewhat familiar voice calling out to her. She ran and jumped into his arms, hugging him at first, and then stepped back, slapping him across the arm. "You were supposed to call me when you got back to town." Allison was glad to see a friend of hers from college who moved away the week after graduation.

Doug Seavers had always said he would sweep her off her feet when she least expected it. She was still secretly waiting. He had been her biggest crush, even though she always knew he and Camille would end up getting married. "I got in late last night. I decided not to wake you up. This morning, I had a meeting. Now I am picking up some things from the dollar store that I didn't want to have to travel with." He pointed to the store, like she did not know where it was. "So do tell, what have you been up to? I'm free for lunch if you want to grab a bite and get caught up."

"That sounds great. I just need to freshen up and change clothes."

"I don't think anyone would care if you wore those tattered, old blue jean shorts and your tank to a nice restaurant. I wouldn't anyway, you still look great, Alli."

"Hush, before I call Camille and tattle on you. I hope you brought pictures."

"Of course! You know I don't go anywhere without my girls." He pulled out his wallet and showed her pictures of Camille and Lacy, their golden retriever. "I have more back at the hotel. Is Rooster's still in business? We could go there now, and plan on a nice dinner this evening, if you do not have plans? My treat. I can subtract part of it."

"That works for me." Allison followed him to Rooster's. They shared stories of the things that had happened since the last time they saw each other and made plans to have dinner later that night. She kissed him goodbye and told him she was looking forward to seeing him again. "And don't forget those pictures. I'll bring some too."

The afternoon flew by, as Allison cleaned the house, put her laundry away, and went through all the pictures she had taken over the last year. She showered and dressed early in case Doug's meeting finished ahead of schedule.

During dinner, Doug told her all about his new job in Chicago. "Camille loves it there. Hopefully, I won't get transferred again for a while. We want to start a family right away, after the wedding."

"I can't believe you guys waited so long to get married."

"Timing! Between jobs and school, we just didn't have the time. But now that things have settled down, we're looking to set the date and start making plans for some time next spring. What about you?"

"I'm not ready for marriage yet. But I'm kind of dating, I guess." Allison told him all about Donovan. "I don't know for sure, but I think he really likes me. I like him too, but his lifestyle is so different than mine. I don't know if we could be together. I can't imagine moving and being on the go all of the time."

"I bet you could never imagine meeting him either, when you first started going to the concerts. Can you stand by now after everything that has happened and let him get away, without even trying to see what it could be?"

Allison knew she would have regrets and spend the rest of her life wondering 'what-if' if she didn't at least give it a try. "I just don't understand why he latched onto me, out of all the people he meets." She had decided to let Donovan know she would go with him, as long as he knew any kind of relationship would have to be taken slowly.

"Well have fun and take lots of pictures! If he lets you?" Doug laughed. They finished dinner and Doug dropped her off, promising to have Camille e-mail as soon as they set the date, so she could make travel plans. He kissed her goodnight, and told her to at least go on the vacation and see how things worked out.

She promised to tell Donovan she would go, the next time she talked to him. "Call me tomorrow morning before you leave. We had lunch and supper; we might as well have breakfast too!"

"I wish there was someone in Miami I could hang out with. I'm going to be there twice as long, and all by myself." Doug was glad to see a familiar face for a change, and would miss not having her to talk to. "It's been fun, Alli. I'll call you in the morning."

Allison slept like a baby, dreaming about her college days, and Doug, and Camille. Her alarm went off bright and early. Time passed quickly as she dressed and waited for Doug to call. She knew his flight was at ten o'clock, so she figured he would want to have breakfast no later than eight thirty. By nine o'clock she was beginning to think he had changed his mind. Allison's phone finally rang about the time she had decided to call him. "It's about time. I was beginning to think you had changed your mind."

A funny voice on the other end surprised her. "Ms. Drexler?"

"I'm sorry. I was expecting a call from someone. I thought you were him."

"Ms. Drexler, I'm sorry to bother you. My name is Sergeant Michaels, ma'am. We got your name from Ms. Camille Winters. She said you were good friends with her and her soon-to-be husband Douglas Seavers, and he mentioned having lunch and dinner with you yesterday. Is that correct ma'am?"

"Yes. Doug and I were supposed to have breakfast this morning too, before he left for Miami, but he hasn't called yet."

"Ms. Winters said we could give you all of the information..."

"Information? What information? What happened? Where's Doug?"

"He was attacked last night in the hotel parking lot. It looks like a robbery. Mr. Seavers was severely beaten and he is in the ICU. We expect a full recovery, but he's going to be sore for a while."

"Do you have any leads? Did you catch the people who did this?" Allison was so upset.

"We are in the process of sorting out all of the details. We'll keep you informed, per Ms. Winter's instructions, until she can get here."

"Can I see him?"

"He's not allowed to have visitors at this time, ma'am.

Can you come down to the station and fill out a report for us, letting us know when you saw him? And answer some questions?"

"Certainly. Anything that might help. I can come right down." Allison grabbed her bag and left for the police station. She was so nervous. She had never been to the police department before. She stopped at the front desk and signed in.

In no time at all, Sergeant Michaels was taking her back to the interrogation room. "Have a seat here Ms. Drexler, the lead officer for the case will be right in." Allison sat quietly, waiting for someone to take all the information she had to offer. She was pleased to see Detective Larson open the door and come in.

"Ms. Drexler, we meet again." Detective Larson sat his paperwork down on his side of the table and reached across to shake hands with her.

"Hello Detective Larson, it's good to see you again. Of course I wish it wasn't under these circumstances. Have you heard how Doug is doing?"

"He's coming around. We think he will be fine. I am sorry about his misfortune. I understand he had been with you earlier in the evening."

"Yes! We had dinner together." Alison was prepared to tell him everything she knew, not that it would be of any use. "Do you want me to tell you everything from the beginning like last time?"

"No. I think we'll do things a little differently this time. What time did Mr. Seavers drop you off?" Detective Larson picked up his pen, turned the page of his notebook and began writing.

"He dropped me off around eight o'clock. We made plans to have breakfast before he left this morning for Miami."

"Did Mr. Seavers hurt you in any way, or make advances towards you?"

Allison was stunned. "What? No! We did not have that kind of relationship! He is getting married! We are only friends. Camille knows that. We are all friends."

"Okay. But you had a crush on him in college?" He waited for a response.

"Yes. I still do. And Camille still knows it, but Doug and I were never more than friends. We never will be. What kind of questions are these, and what do they have to do with Doug being robbed?"

"Ms. Drexler, I assure you, these are just part of the ongoing investigation including Mr. Seavers. I didn't mean to imply that anything was going on between the two of you, I only wanted to make sure I had all of the facts correct."

"The facts are simple. I knew Doug was coming to town; Camille called me a few weeks ago. Doug was supposed to call when he got here, but we ran into each other yesterday in the parking lot before he got a chance to call. We went for a quick lunch at Rooster's and made plans to have a nice dinner at The Lobster House. He picked me up around six. We shared pictures, stories and talked through dinner, getting caught up. He dropped me off around eight. No more, no less. Your Sergeant Michaels called this morning and told me Doug had been robbed and beaten up. That's all I know."

"Okay, Ms. Drexler. I just need to get the paperwork filled out and have you sign it. We appreciate all your help in this matter. I'll be back in just a minute." Detective Larson stepped outside the room and was talking to Sergeant Michaels. "I tell you Sarge, I don't think she had anything to do with this. She didn't beat her coworker, she didn't kill Mr. Landon, and she didn't beat Mr. Seavers up either." Drake was certain Allison was innocent, or at least he really wanted her to be. "I know what it looks like, but I don't think she had anything to do with this."

"I know it doesn't seem possible, but this is the fourth incident linked to Ms. Drexler. Remember a few months ago when we had that kid come in reporting he had been assaulted. He had been going out with Ms. Drexler again for almost a week when someone beat the shit out of him and left him for dead."

"Yes, but she doesn't even know about the beatings until after we tell her about them."

"We never questioned her in the Connor Everett beating? He swore she didn't have anything to do with it."

"And I believe him. She was terrified after the Landon murder. She even confessed, thinking she had accidentally killed him. I was there! I saw her reaction. I know something is going on, but I don't know what. And when we do figure this out, I know you'll see I'm right about this girl."

"Okay Larson. Let her go, for now. But let her know we may need to have her answer some more questions. I am going to set a tail up on her and see where she goes, who she sees. If she had someone do this, they'll need to meet up at some point."

Drake told Allison she could go. "Thanks again for all of your help. I understand Ms. Winters is at the hospital now and that she has been asking for you."

"Thank you. So can I go, see them now?"

"Yes. I think it is okay for you to visit. I may need to contact you if I need more information."

"Of course! Anytime. Just let me know." Allison shook hands with Detective Larson. "I'm glad it was you I got to talk with today. I liked having someone that I already knew. Did you work last night? Is that how you were assigned to Doug's case?"

"Yes. It's been a long night."

"I'm sure it has been. I for one wish this had never happened. Poor Doug. He is strong. He will pull through this. Good luck finding the guy who did this."

"Thank you, Ms. Drexler, a little luck might come in handy."

Chapter Seven

Allison left the police station and went straight to the hospital. Camille was sitting in the waiting room, outside of the ICU. "Camille? Is he okay?"

Camille stood up, giving her a big hug. Both girls started crying. "I can't believe this happened." They sat down, gaining their composure.

"I know. How is he doing this morning?"

"He's sore. They are cleaning him up right now. He wanted me to do it, but the nurse said he had too many lines and they couldn't risk having something being pulled out." The girls talked while they waited for the nurse to let them know it was okay to come back in. Camille told her Doug was still traveling a lot, but at the beginning of the year he was going to be able to stay home most of the time. "He called me as soon as he left The Lobster House last night and gave me your e-mail address. I hung up earlier than usual so I could e-mail you. You should have an e-mail." Camille started crying again. "If I had stayed on the phone, maybe this wouldn't have happened."

"He still would have gotten to the hotel the same time he did. The robbers probably wouldn't have cared that he was on the phone. So do not think like that. Or I could say it was my fault for going out with him."

"Okay, stop. Neither one of us caused this, or could have stopped it. But he's going to be all right and that's all that matters." The nurse called out to have the visitor's assistant send Camille back. Doug was glad to see Allison too. "Sorry I missed breakfast."

Allison started bawling. She flung herself over Doug hugging him, apologizing. "I'm so sorry this happened."

Doug hugged her, the best he could. He smiled up at Camille. "Now I have my two favorite girls here with me. I couldn't be better."

Allison raised her head up. "Don't let Lacy hear you say that."

Doug laughed, coughing, moaning out in pain. "Don't make me laugh. It hurts too much."

"And you couldn't be better? Right!" Allison was glad to see he was going to be okay.

"I'll go, so you two can visit, and so you can rest. And you better do everything the nurses tell you to." She invited Camille to stay at the apartment and told her to call if she needed anything. That evening, Allison and Camille baked a bunch of goodies to take to the hospital. They were having a lot of fun, until someone knocked on the door and they jumped.

Allison looked out to see Detective Larson. He smiled. Allison looked down to see how she looked, then opened the door. "Ms. Drexler, I saw the lights were on and wanted to check to see how your friend was doing." Allison asked him to come in. He was surprised to see Camille there.

"Oh? Hello Ms. Winters, it is a pleasure to see you again. It smells good in here."

"We're baking. We're going to take some things up to the hospital tomorrow." Allison busied herself making a to-go baggy for the detective. Camille told the detective how Doug was doing and asked if they had any leads in the case.

"We are following some leads, and collecting as much evidence as we can. Security tapes from the hotel, witnesses; hopefully we'll be able to wrap this up before you leave to go back to Chicago."

Allison gave the bag full of goodies to Detective Larson. "I made this for you. I hope you get a chance to enjoy it tonight. I know you keep busy."

"Thank you, Ms. Drexler. But I really shouldn't."

"Oh please! It will keep me from bringing them to the station and having to hunt you down. See? You're saving me the trip this way." Allison insisted.

"Sounds like a good enough reason to me. I better go. I am glad to hear Mr. Seavers is doing well. Thank you for the sweets, ladies. Lock the door behind me."

The following morning the girls packed a basket and took the sweets to the hospital. Allison left Camille there and went to work. Donovan called that afternoon early. Allison told him she was ready to say yes to the vacation if he still wanted to go. Of course he was excited and said he would let her know when and where just as soon as he figured it out for sure.

Allison was having a good day. After her lunch with Madison, Camille called her and told her they were moving Doug out of the ICU and that he might be released tomorrow. Allison was so happy she even agreed to have dinner with Trenton, so she could tell him everything that had happened.

During dinner, Trenton got a little agitated. "I think we need to call that detective friend of yours and fill him in."

"Trent, what on earth are you talking about?"

"I'm worried about you."

"About me? Why?"

Trenton told her someone had approached him in the parking lot after work one night several months ago. "He kept saying I better stay away from her, if I know what's good for me. I had no idea what he was talking about. But now, I think he was talking about you."

"Me? Someone warned you to stay away from me? That doesn't make any sense! Why on earth? Who on earth would do that?"

"I don't know, but that's not all. Sometime earlier this year, or the end of last year, I don't remember, I saw someone taking pictures of you."

"What?"

"Well I convinced myself I had to be mistaken. They must have been taking pictures of something else. But remember when I said I followed you to the party that night? I saw someone else. I didn't think a whole lot about it until this morning coming into work. I think I saw the same person taking pictures of you again."

"Trenton! Why didn't you say something earlier?" Allison flipped through her bag looking for Detective Larson's number.

"I didn't know if I was right or not. But after hearing about someone else you went out with getting beaten up, I don't have doubts anymore." Trenton apologized.

Allison called Detective Larson and told him they needed to talk to him right away. She told him she thought she was being followed and didn't know if she should come to the station or not. She explained what Trenton told her over the phone, and asked what they should do.

"I'm afraid we need to protect your friend. If what he said is true, then he is a target right now. Take him with you to the hospital. I'll meet you in the lobby, and I'll be in plain clothes." Detective Larson was already waiting when they got to the hospital. "I called Sergeant Michaels and told him what you said and asked him what he thought we should do." He told them the Sergeant wanted to add a tail to Trenton in case someone tried to attack him.

"What about me?" Allison was beginning to panic.

"Well, you need a new boyfriend." Detective Larson stood up and held his hand out like he was meeting her for the first time. "Hello. I guess we should probably start using first names at this point. My name is Drake Larson, your new boyfriend. Sarge said since I had already been by your place a few times, that it would be believable enough for us to start dating."

Allison shook his hand. "Hello new boyfriend, my name is Allison." Drake hugged her and kissed her on the cheek.

"Just in case he's watching. That might take some of the attention off of Mr. Stewart."

Trenton pouted. "But he already warned me. Wouldn't it make more sense for me to be the boyfriend? He's already seen us together."

"We can't take a chance on something happening to you." Detective Larson asked the visitor's assistant if there was a conference room they could borrow, where he could take Trenton's statement, without fear of being watched. She led them into the ICU and down a hallway, behind the supply room.

Trenton told him everything he had told Allison earlier. "So now what?"

"Let me call the Sergeant and see if we have someone in place to watch you."

Trenton took Allison's hand. He could tell she was worried. "I'll be all right. Do not worry. You will be fine too. You are going to be in good hands." Trenton liked Drake a lot more than he liked Donovan.

"Okay! Someone is in place and waiting at the mall parking lot. They will follow you home after Ms... after Allison drops you off. And they will go everywhere you go until we catch this guy. As for us, I will come by your apartment later, before I have to go to work."

Trenton started getting upset quickly. "That's great! Someone is going to be tailing me, and you're going to just leave her to fend for herself. Don't you think..."

"Someone has been tailing Allison since she left the police station the other day." He turned to Allison, apologizing. "I'll explain later. So, do you want to go up and see Mr. Seavers before we go? But don't say anything to him about this!"

Doug was glad to see them. He looked so much better. "I feel great. I'm ready to get the heck outta here."

Allison reached down to tickle him. "Until you laugh again."

"Don't! I am better. I might actually get to go home tomorrow."

Drake asked him to stick around for a few days and see if the leads they were working on produced a suspect.

"We're staying in town until the end of the week. And his boss is paying for it." Camille was glad to know they didn't have to try to hurry and fly home, or rush to Miami so Doug could make all those meetings.

"Call me and let me know for sure about tomorrow. I should be able to leave work to pick you up." Allison felt terrible knowing that all of this happened because of her. And they were just friends. Someone neglected to do their research. The more she thought about it, the madder she got.

Chapter Eight

Allison dropped Trenton off at his car, in the mall parking lot. Trenton was looking around. "Stop looking like you are looking for someone. We don't want him to know we are on to him." Allison just shook her head, wondering how this was ever going to work. "And be careful. I'll see you tomorrow at work." Thoughts raced through her mind, as her imagination took over. Who would be watching her, and why would they hurt her friends? She hoped this would all be over very soon. Partly because she really did not like the idea of being watched, but more because she wanted to know who was doing the watching.

Allison had only been home a few minutes when Detective Larson pulled in. She ran to the door. She wrapped her arms around his neck, and kissed him. He lifted her up into his arms, carrying her inside, closing the door behind him. Allison was disappointed when he sat her down and backed away apologizing.

"I'm sorry Ms. Drex... Allison. But if they followed you, instead of Trenton that should convince them we're more than just friends." He turned the lights off.

Allison had liked this man from the first moment she

laid eyes on him. And now he was in her apartment, as her boyfriend. "I thought you'd be in uniform?"

"I don't wear a uniform anymore, and it's better if the person didn't know he was attacking a member of the police department. It might mean the difference between just getting beaten up like everyone else so far or being shot to death."

Allison shivered at the thought. "Don't talk like that. You are not going to be beaten up. You are going to beat him up. And then I am going to…"

"Careful! You don't want to say anything that might get you in trouble." Drake led her to the couch. "May I sit down?"

"Oh, certainly! Where are my manors? Can I get you something to drink?" Allison headed into the kitchen.

Drake followed. "Ms. Dr… Allison, you have a nice little place here." He helped her pour the lemonade.

"Do you want some popcorn or anything?"

"Sure. Sergeant Michaels and I think it would be a good idea for me to spend the night." Thank God the bowl Allison was getting out of the cabinet was plastic, because she dropped it. Drake picked it up, taking her hand. "This guy has been very aggressive. We think it is only a matter of time before he starts letting himself be known to you. And then God only knows what he will do. He is obviously very possessive." They finished popping the popcorn and went back to the couch.

Allison turned the TV on, but turned the volume down so they could talk. "So, what do we do next?"

"Sarge said I should let you in on everything that has

happened; everything that we've been able to piece together anyway… since you're no longer a suspect."

"That's why you had me followed from the station!" Allison almost cried at the thought of being a suspect.

"Not me! The Sarge! There are things you don't even know about." Drake took a deep breath. "We do a lot of cross-referencing at the station. When something happens, we type the names of the people involved into the computer to see what else, if anything, they have been involved in. When Mr. Landon died and we started the investigation, your name came up from the party, and the incident you reported. We cross-referenced your name, and several other events were listed throughout the year."

Allison was horrified. "What? My name turned up several events? Oh my Gosh! I can't even imagine."

"Each incident listed was for an assault case."

"Like Doug's?"

"Yes. The first one was around a year ago. Do you remember if you were seeing someone, or if you met someone you might want to start seeing?" Drake took out his pen and paper. The casual evening turned to work. "A year ago? I have to try to remember everything that happened the whole year." Allison had never wished she kept a diary before, but one would certainly come in handy right now. "A year ago… I was seeing my ex-boyfriend around that time. Connor and I had dated for over a year and broke up. We separated for months, but Connor wanted to get back together. We tried dating again, but it didn't work and we went our separate ways."

"Did you break it off with him?"

"Yes. He had a drinking problem."

"Ms. Drexler, …"

"Allison!"

"Allison, Connor was assaulted the day he asked you to reconsider the final break-up."

"Oh my God! How badly was he hurt?"

"He had to go to the emergency room. When he reported having been beaten, the police had to be notified. He mentioned your name. That's how your name was associated with the case."

"But no one ever questioned me about it."

"Mr. Everett had been drinking, and it wasn't the first time he had gotten into a fight while he was drunk. At that point you were not a suspect. There was no reason to question you." Drake felt bad having to tell her all of this. But she had to know. Hopefully, something would trigger an idea about who might be following her. Drake continued. "A couple of weeks after that, a Tony Norman was convinced that you had sent someone to beat him up after he made advances towards you at a bar earlier that night."

"Tony Norman?" Allison did not recognize the name.

"Yes. He said he met you at a Silverman's Saloon."

"Silverman's? I haven't been there since that twerp, Anthony, oh shit! That's him. Anthony. He was trying to be so professional. Said he was a lawyer. Short. Dark, thinning hair. Greasy. A pervert! He got pissed because I wouldn't dance with him. He was very persistent, and kept grabbing my arm, and putting his arm around me, grabbing my butt! I slapped him and told him to get lost. He still wouldn't leave me alone. I left. I haven't been back there since. I am not fond of the bar scene!"

"Mr. Norman had a rap-sheet. I actually think he's in jail now, for sexual harassment."

"Good! He should be!"

"And Tom Galloway, he actually works with you. How is he doing? Is he back to work yet?"

"Yes. He's still sore, and taking it slow, but we let him come back to work. He and Jillie are barely scraping by." Allison shook her head in disbelief. "So, you're telling me that all of these guys were beaten up, some so much they were hospitalized all because of me?"

"When Mr. Landon turned up dead after attacking you, and it was the fourth time your name turned up with similar cases, we had to consider the fact that you could be involved. Not doing it yourself, but that you may have someone doing it for you."

"Well, I can certainly see why you would have to consider me a suspect. Scary though, to think all of this was going on, and I didn't even know about it. So it looks like all of these cases may well be connected, and because of me."

"Yes, but now we have to find out who, and why! We have a time-line to go by." Drake pulled out a graph with all of the incidents listed. "Can you think of anything that happened prior to the first attack?"

Allison studied the graph. She tore one of Drake's sheets of paper out and started tracking her life over the last couple of years. Work, concerts, going out every so often, but nothing seemed to stand out.

"Did you move? Meet someone new?" Drake tried to help her think of things that had happened. "Do you go to the same grocery store, where someone has been flirting with you?" Allison shook her head, thinking of all the places she goes to on a regular basis. She jotted them all down. "Does anyone come to see you at work? Do you ever notice someone watching you when you go down for lunch? Has Ms. Cannon ever mentioned feeling like she was being watched?"

"No! Nothing. I am not helping. I am sorry! This is freaking me out. It could be anyone, and I wouldn't even know it." Allison started to cry.

Drake scooted closer to her, putting his arm across her shoulder for moral support. "I am sorry this is happening, but we'll figure it out. He's getting lazy, even Trenton saw him taking pictures and knew he was following you." He took her face in his hands. "For now, we have to consider everyone a possible suspect. You cannot tell anyone about the investigation. Okay." He reached out turning the TV back up and changed the channel. "That's enough for now. Let's take a break!" They watched TV for a while. Drake changed the subject, asking her about her job. What she did all day as an assistant manager? How long she had worked there? He told her he wanted to be a police officer in the second grade, when an officer came to the school to do his speech about not talking to strangers and staying close to your parents. He watched all of the police shows growing up and read all of the books he could about law enforcement. Drake excused himself to the bathroom when Allison's phone rang.

Donovan was calling to see how she was doing and tell her about the concert in Las Vegas. "Dillon almost fell off the front of the stage. He went into one of his slides, and couldn't stop. It was so funny. We messed the song up so bad, we just stopped singing it. We took turns sliding on the floor for a while before we started singing again."

"I'm sorry I missed it!"

"We always tape the shows, so I'll see if I can't get you a copy! And there is always the internet!"

"Are you serious? Do you have copies of all of the concerts you've ever done? That would make for a really nice gift for someone!"

"Only if she was trust-worthy and we knew they wouldn't end up on the internet or anything. We have to be careful, you know!"

"I do know. But how cool would that be? Maybe not every single concert, just the ones like last night when something happens. And one that was perfect, so we could have something to compare it too." Allison went into the kitchen to refill the lemonade. "Well, I'm glad Dillon is okay. Have a safe trip to California."

"I miss you. I wish you could fly out. There are only three more shows left. Then we have a week off before we go to Europe. Two weeks in Europe and then we're done, until we head back to the studio."

"Madison and I talked about trying to fly out there. Will we be able to get in without a ticket? And can we stay with you if we do?"

"You know it. Just say the word!"

"Okay. We'll check our schedules and see how much money we have in savings."

"Money? You won't need any money. I will book the flights too. The only money you will need is if you want to buy something. All you need is time."

"That's probably going to be harder to get than the

money." Allison laughed and told him she would talk to him more about it later. She hung up, and took the lemonades back into the living room. "I'm sorry about that. Do you want something else to snack on? I didn't even think to ask you if you had eaten dinner."

"Yes, I ate dinner, and no, I don't need anything else. I am good. So, was that your boyfriend?" Drake was curious to know if she was seeing anyone at the time. He had thoughts of asking her out after all of this was over.

"Nope! I am not really serious with anyone right now. That was just Donovan, the bass player from Dillonsledge, we are kind of dating. Madi and I have been to several concerts, and got to meet them. Now Donovan and Derek call us all of the time. We hang out with them sometimes after the concerts. Donovan invited me to go on a vacation after he finishes his tour. Just now, he said he'd pay for us to fly out and catch the show in California if we could get off from work."

"Dillonsledge? Are you serious? You mean I know someone who knows them?"

"Yep!" Allison laughed. 'Knows them' is one way to put it.

"Wow! But you are not his girlfriend and he's paying for you to go all the way out there?"

"That's what he just said. He called to tell me Dillon almost slid off the, front of the stage tonight. They are so crazy."

"So how long have you been seeing him, or hanging out with them?"

"We went to two concerts during their first tour. We met them backstage before the second concert. One thing led to another. It is hard to believe we have been hanging around with them for two years already! "

"So do you think it will lead to seriously dating?" He was really asking for personal reasons, but also needed to know professionally. After all, everyone was a suspect at this point. He made a note to check their tour schedule.

Chapter Nine

Allison yawned. "I am so sorry. I guess all of this is wearing me out."

"And you have to work in the morning. I should let you go to sleep." Drake did not want her to leave, but he stood up, pulling her up with him. He softly slid the hair out of her face. "Allison, after all of this is over, would it be all right for me to…" His phone rang. "I'm sorry, I have to take this."

Allison went to the bedroom and changed. Drake was still on the phone and waiting for her. "The guys on stake-out just called and said someone suspicious drove by slowly. They said he is turning around and coming back. I need to go to my car." He turned the phone off. "Come with me." He opened the door, and then turned around and kissed her, for the second time tonight. He whispered for her to stay in the doorway and patted her on the butt as he turned to go to the car. He grabbed a duffle bag out of the car and ran back inside. He threw the duffle bag through the door and started kissing her again, as the car passed by. He picked her up and carried her inside again and slammed the door. He carried her to the couch.

Allison felt the same kind of adrenaline rush in those

fake kisses as she did after the concerts. Drake's ringing phone brought her back into the moment at hand. He was all smiles. "Good! We just caught the break we needed. The car that turned around was also taking pictures."

"Did they arrest the guy?" Allison was glad to know this whole thing would soon be over.

"They can't arrest him for driving slowly and taking pictures. They got the make, model, and tags. We can look him up and see if he has priors. But we'll have to wait and see if he does something else."

"I never did understand that. Wait until they do something before you can talk to them? Can't you pick him up for questioning about the other cases?"

"Yes, technically. But we do not want him to know we are on to him. Right now, we have the edge. He is going to mess up, and when he does, we're going to be right there. We have a picture of him now too, and the license plate number. They are running it as we speak." Allison was so excited, she jumped into his arms. It suddenly got awkward.

Mutually he let her down. He half –heartedly hugged her, knowing she had Donovan issues to work through, and he was working… timing, it was all about timing. "So, what I was saying earlier, depending on what you decide to do, or not to do with Donovan, do you think after this is over, I could ask you out, if you and Donovan aren't really serious yet by then?"

"Does that mean I can never go to another Dillonsledge concert?"

"No. It just means you have to take me with you." Drake sat down on the couch, inviting her to sit down with him. "Do you have time to watch TV before you have to go to bed?" He flipped to one of the late-night talk shows and got comfortable with Allison lying in his arms.

Allison loved how he felt. She loved him being from Daytona. She loved how he made her feel safe. She dozed off.

Drake changed into a pair of shorts and a t-shirt and turned the sheets down on Allison's bed. She finally woke up as he was laying her on the bed. "I'm sorry. I was going to let you stay out there with me, but when I got up to change, you stretched out on the whole couch. I didn't think it was right to stay in here while you were out there."

"You can stay in here now." Allison knew that was not a good idea. "Just on the bed I mean, instead of the couch. On your side!"

Drake bent in and kissed her. "As much as I'd like to stay, I can't do that, not yet anyway." He turned to leave. "Do you want the door opened?"

"Yes. Drake… thank you for everything you are doing for me. And for giving me the time I need to figure out how I really feel about Donovan."

"I'm glad to help." He turned the light off. "See you in the morning." Allison tossed and turned and had not gotten much sleep before the alarm went off. She showered, dressed, and made breakfast while Drake slept. She fixed his plate and sat it on the coffee table. She turned the TV on, hoping that would wake him up. She was sitting cross-legged in the recliner when he finally opened his eyes.

She picked up her plate and started eating. "I didn't know what you liked, so I gave you a little bit of everything. There's more in the kitchen if you want it."

He sat up, pulling the blanket over his protruding shorts.

"This will be fine." He picked the plate up and scooted back. "So how did you sleep?"

"I didn't sleep very much. How 'bout you?"

"New noises and all, so not very good, I jumped every time I heard something. I was hoping to get a good night's sleep, so I would be ready for anything that might happen today. The attacker usually strikes right away. So that means he will probably follow me home, or wherever I go. I have to call the Sergeant and find out what he wants me to do. I'm sure they already have a staging area all set up."

Allison could not take it anymore. She sat her plate down and stood up. She caught him completely off guard.

"What are you doing?"

She threw the blanket onto the floor. "Throwing caution to the wind? Or instead, just sending you to the shower before I do something we both might regret." She grabbed his plate of food. "You'll have to heat this up or pick something up on the way to work!"

After a quick shower, Drake called the Sergeant.

Allison finished getting ready for work, and heated what was left of their breakfast. "What did he say?"

Drake took his plate and sat down at the kitchen table. "You get to go to work with one tail. I get to leave with everybody else. The guy who has been following you has a rap sheet a mile long. One of the lady detectives will be bringing you a picture and everything we have on the guy. She will be posing as a candidate for employment coming in for an interview. Obviously, you will be the one doing the honors. She's also going to do a sweep of the office, to see if there are any bugs. I checked here last night, but didn't find anything."

"Do they have a place all set up for you to go to?"

"They have me going to a safe house. If I make it that far, I'll change into my work shirt and pants and go to the video store at the mall where I work. They left a Videos Plus T-shirt with my name tag and khaki pants for me. I'll take an hour for lunch and come to see you. What do you want for lunch? I'll stop and get it so we can eat upstairs."

"A fish sandwich and a loaded baked potato, and a banana smoothie. Do I need to write that down, or can you remember?" Allison was laughing. "I'm only kidding, anything is fine."

"Fish, potatoes, and bananas it is! What time should I be there?"

"What time is your friend coming? Do you have any idea?"

"They didn't say. But I imagine that it will be this morning. You should take something for lunch, just in case. Or if I'm not there by twelve, you can have lunch with Ms. Cannon."

"You can call her Madi. I do!" Allison was certain she would not care. They finished breakfast and left for work. Drake walked her to her car, giving her a big kiss, squeezing her butt. Allison wondered if he was like this all the time, or if it was all for show.

Allison stopped by to see Madison on her way to work. She told her everything that had happened. Madison was just as shocked as Allison was. Allison started to tell her about what Donovan had said about the concert, but Madison already knew about it.

"Derek called me last night and filled me in. He said he wanted us to come to the last show and wanted to know if we were going to be able to get off work. Are you still going to try to go?"

"I don't know. Drake asked me last night if he could ask me out after all of this was over."

"Well I guess you gave him an answer?" Madison got all shy. "I have my own little thing going on. With Derek. Well, kind of. He asked me last night if he could come and stay with me a while after the tour is over."

Allison squealed. "Oh my Gosh! Like how excited are you?" Allison put her finger up to Madison's lips. "Duh! Don't answer that." She gave Madison a big hug. "Enjoy! But take it slow. I don't want you to get hurt, so keep the right attitude. Okay?"

Madison promised. She told Allison she would come to Shiley's for lunch today. "I'll call you later and see when you can get away."

Allison stopped by Mr. Gillespie's office next, and told him what the police had found out. She also let him know an officer was coming by for an interview later, and would be sweeping the place for bugs. Mr. Gillespie said Sergeant Michaels had already called and filled him in.

Chapter Ten

Allison had hoped she would be better at this than she was. She decided she could never be an actress. She moved around the sales floor, changing out signs, straightening merchandise, suspecting every customer. Mr. Gillespie finally persuaded her to retreat to her office and work on the next schedule. It was nine-thirty when the cashier finally overhead paged for Allison to come to the front of the store, but it seemed much later. She prayed with all of her might that it would be the undercover officer and not some man she didn't recognize. She stopped and called the cashier to see who it was before she left. "Okay. Thanks. Tell her I will be right there."

Allison was pleased to hear the officer had arrived. She could not wait to see pictures of this guy and find out if it was someone she actually knew. "Hello. My name is Allison Drexler, assistant manager. It's a pleasure to have you here today."

"Thank you. I am Nancy Lawrence. I'm really excited about the possibility of coming to work with you." The officer was dressed in a skirt, with a button-down dress shirt.

She reached into her bag and handed Allison a resume. "I hope you find my extensive work history to be a plus."

"From what you said on the phone, I'm sure it will be. So, what brings you to Shiley's?" Okay, so maybe she could be an actress after all. The two traded small talk on the way to the office.

The officer continued the fake interview process until she had a chance to check the place out. "Okay, Ms. Drexler, I didn't find anything in here." She shook hands with Allison and re-introduced herself. "Hello again, my name is Detective Truman. I have the information on the man that has been following you." She pulled out all of the paperwork and started filling Allison in. "His name is Walter Shannon. He has priors in Georgia and South Carolina, as well as Florida. He has served time for sexual assault and battery, and for robbery.

Allison was speechless. The name did not sound familiar. She could not remember ever being so scared. "Who is he, and what does he want with me?"

"We don't know right now, but we will find out." Detective Truman was very sympathetic and optimistic.

"Do you know if he followed Detective Larson this morning? Or have you heard anything?"

"He followed Larson back to the safe house, took some pictures and then left. He drove past your car here at the mall, and then went back to the safe house. We have reason to believe he has something different in mind for Larson." The officer had a scared look on her face.

"Why do you say that?"

"According to the files we have on record, he usually attacks your... he usually attacks right away, as soon as possible. We really thought he would have tried something this morning. But he did not, so Larson is at the other end of the mall, at the video store, acting as a manager. We can only hope this works. It all depends on how closely he followed you and just how much he knows." The detective's phone rang. Allison patiently waited, trying not to read anything into the one-sided conversation she was hearing. "It appears our suspect is trying to get more information on Larson. He came back to the mall and is on his way into the video store. Sarge wants you to go down and visit Larson. We have the video cameras from the store surveillance and several undercover agents on their way. Do you think you can do this?"

"Why do I have to go down there, shouldn't we just wait and see what he does with Lar… Drake?" Allison was not only scared to death, but afraid she would give something away and scare him off, and then she would never know. Or given the right mood, she might just have to ask him herself, if everybody else was just going to pussy-foot around it. She really did not want to go.

"We closed the store this morning. The only people inside are working undercover. We cannot afford to blow this and have to risk staging another meeting somewhere else. This Mr. Shannon took the bait. He is on his way to the store right now. Think of this as adding fuel to the fire. He has never seen you two together and wants to know if it is a one-time thing or not. He wants to know if he has a reason to attack Larson. We need to give him that reason. The sooner he attacks Larson, the sooner we may be able to find something out." Allison grabbed her purse and was halfway out the door.

The detective stopped her. "Act natural. We do not want to set off any red flags with this guy. This will give us a chance to see how he reacts to being close to you. And do not encourage eye contact, try not to notice him. You're there to see Larson." Detective Truman stayed back in the center of the mall, out of sight. Allison entered the video store through the mall. She immediately noticed Drake behind the counter, getting cash out of the register. Drake shot her a look when he heard the door open and looked back at Mr. Shannon. She followed Drake's eyes to the man that had been following her. Walter Shannon had a gun pointed at Drake and was in the process of robbing the store.

Allison screamed. "No!" Shots were fired and Allison fell to the floor. She heard screaming.

"Don't kill him. We need him to tell us why he's following Ms. Drexler."

Detective Truman heard the shots and rushed to Allison's side. "Oh my God, are you okay?"

"He shot Drake!" Allison was bawling. She tried to run to the counter, but Truman would not let her.

"I'm okay!" Drake moaned. He pushed his way through the crowd and wrapped his arms around her. He raised his shirt opened to a bullet-proof vest with a bullet half sticking out of it. "I'm okay. Let's get you out of here."

"But you're the lead detective on my case, you have to take that bastard to the station and find out why in the…" Allison collapsed in Drake's arms as he kissed her.

"I'm so glad this is over! Now we can find out what's going on." Drake raised his shoulder, in agonizing pain. He took his shirt the rest of the way off and pulled his arm through one side of the vest and then the other. He pitched the vest over to Truman. "Make sure this gets to the department. I am going to take Ms. Drexler back to Shiley's. I'll be back at the station in a little while." Drake walked Allison down the mall. He detoured towards the food court.

"What are you doing?" Allison wanted him to get back to the station. "I'm getting you that fish sandwich and loaded baked potato."

"No, you're not! I brought my lunch. And besides, I am not going to be able to eat. I just saw you get shot!" Allison started crying.

"I was kind of hoping this could be our first date."

"But you're not going to ask me out until you get this all taken care of. Remember? And until I decide whether or not I want to be with Donovan."

He kissed her again. "Oh? Well, I guess I better get you back to work then, so I can wrap this up. As for Donovan, I've decided not to let him win without a fight." He walked her back to her office and told Mr. Gillespie to keep an eye on her.

Mr. Gillespie asked if he could speak with him, and led Drake to his office. "I didn't know if I should say anything in front of Allison or not. This morning, we got an anonymous tip that Allison was stealing from the store. I know she would never do anything like that, and I told the gentleman on the other end of the phone he was mistaken. He insisted and said we should fire her if we knew what was good for us. I told him if she were stealing from the store and we could prove it, she would be brought up on charges. He hung up."

"Did he give you any indication as to who he was?" Drake wrote down everything Mr. Gillespie could remember.

"I'll have someone see if we can track the num. say anything to Allison."

Drake told Allison to stay in the office until they sure this guy was working alone. "We can't take any chanc There are two officers here." He pointed to the man standing at the bottom of the stairs. "There is another one on the floor. And do not talk about anything that has happened until the case is closed. For now, everyone is still a suspect."

Allison heard her phone ringing. "Should I get that?"

"See who it is? Do you recognize the number?"

"It's Donovan."

"Oh? He'll call back." He kissed her on the cheek, waving to the phone. "Answer it. I'm kidding." He left her talking to Donovan and gave strict orders to the man at the bottom of the stairs to keep an eye on her.

Allison waved goodbye and answered the phone. "Hello?" She was afraid she had missed his call.

"Hello? I thought you got tired of me and moved on."

"My bag was on the other side of the room, I almost didn't hear the phone ring, and then I couldn't find my phone. What are you doing?"

"Calling to see if I should book a flight for you and Madison. Derek told me he invited Madison to come out here for the last show."

Allison interrupted him. "About that, I don't think I'm going to be able to come?"

"Sure, you can, just tell your boss you're taking off to come see me. He likes me. Remember? Should I talk to him again?"

"No. Madison hasn't said yet if she is even going to be

t off work. Why don't we leave it at… if we can
, we will be there; if we can't, we won't."

That's no way to leave things. I hear Derek is coming
see Madison after the tour is over. I still haven't gotten
an invitation." He waited for a response. "I'm not trying to
rush you into anything. I just want to spend time with you."

"I know, Donovan. There is just so much going on right
now. I need to let you go Donovan. I'm sorry." Allison hung
up. She hated just hanging up on him like that, and she
wished she could tell him everything, but he would have to
wait. Hopefully he would understand when this was all over,
and she was finally able to tell him.

Chapter Eleven

Allison had lunch in her office with Madison and filled her in. "Donovan was so upset this afternoon. I had to hang up and couldn't tell him anything."

"He'll understand when you tell him what's been going on. Has Drake called to let you know what he found out?" Madison was so glad her friend didn't get hurt in the shoot out.

"No. He hasn't called." Allison picked at her food. "I can't believe this character is someone I don't even know. Like how did he find me? What made him pick me out to stalk?"

"That is so spooky! It makes my skin crawl just thinking about it. And how long has he been watching you? We don't even know that." Madison finished eating and said she needed to get back to work. "Let me know as soon as you hear something."

Allison was restless the rest of the afternoon. She imagined a thousand scenarios in her head trying to figure out how this Mr. Shannon knew her. Drake finally called and said he would meet her at her apartment after work. She could not wait to find out about this Mr. Shannon and see just what it was about her that had caught his interest enough to make him hurt the people around her. She was making herself crazy with worry.

Drake was waiting for her when she got home. "I'm afraid I don't really have much to tell you. The guy's not talking. When we asked him why he was stalking you and taking pictures of you, he said he didn't know what we were talking about, that we must have him confused with someone else."

Allison started crying, and then got stark-raving-mad. She was relieved when they took this guy into custody, thinking that would be the end of everything. "Did your guys from the stake out show him their pictures?"

"He still denied having anything to do with hurting any of the guys. The only thing we've charged him with right now is robbery and attempted murder." Drake was sorry he did not have better news. "At least we know he won't be following you anymore. And we are following all our leads. Trenton will be a big help tomorrow if he can identify Shannon as the man that warned him to stay away from you."

"That's good. But will that be enough?"

"We are also bringing in Doug and Connor to positively identify him. Doug's the most important witness we have right now."

"Camille called from the hotel and said your officers picked them up from the hospital this afternoon and that you have a guard outside their hotel door. Do you really think there is more than one person involved, that he may not be in on this alone?" Allison's fears resurfaced.

"It's always a possibility, so we can't be too careful.

Tomorrow you will go to work like always, as will I. Hopeful. by the end of the day we will have more information and everything we need to book this guy. But tonight, I am staying here!" Drake threw the blanket he used from the night before back up onto the couch.

"Okay Drake! But you don't have to stay out here, if you don't want to." Allison was scared and would not mind having him as close as possible. After supper, Allison showered and laid her clothes out for the following morning. Drake was watching TV when she came out. She sat down on the couch with him, noticing the bruise from the gun shot earlier."How's your bullet wound?"

"It's still a little tender. I had no idea what he was up to when I saw him come in, but we think he had every intention of killing me. That he wanted it to look like a robbery gone bad." Drake was worried for Allison's sake. "If this guy thought for a second that we may be onto him, or even if he didn't, he would need to start covering his tracks. He already had numerous incidents tied to you. He would have to do something different, to keep us from linking all of the murders and assaults back to you. There's no telling what else he's done that we don't even know about." Allison stared blankly into space. Drake softly rubbed the back of his hand against her face, turned her face towards him and then kissed her forehead. He wanted to protect her at any cost. He promised her she would be safe, and that he would not let anything happen to her. He told her he would stay with her as long as she wanted him to.

"I want you to hold me all night. I am scared Drake!" She shot him a glance to see if he believed her or not. "I

an that. I am not just saying that so you will sleep with
me either!"

Drake laughed. "I didn't think anything like that. And
as much as I would like to 'sleep with you' I think I should
stay out here again tonight."

Allison put her night clothes on and brushed her teeth.
She grabbed her pillow from the bed and curled up on the
couch with Drake.

"What are you doing?"

"Well, since you're staying out here, so am I." Allison
got comfortable and closed her eyes.

"Oh no you're not! Now go to bed." Drake pulled her
pillow out from under her head.

"Drake? I really am afraid. I don't think I can sleep. I
want you near me, even if it has to be out here."

Drake sighed, giving her pillow back to her. "Fine,
then we'll sleep in there. But sleep! That is all, understand?
Tonight, and in the morning, just sleep." Sleep did not come
easy, for either one of them. And when it did, their dreams
were not kind.

Drake was up making coffee already when the alarm
went off. Neither one spoke a word during breakfast. When
Drake dropped her off at her office door, he finally told
her he would call her if there was a break in the case. "The
guards are going to be here every day, until we figure out
whether or not this guy was working alone. Can you go to
Madison's after work, if I do not make it back here in time
to pick you up?"

"I'm sure Madison won't mind. I'll call her to see if she
has other plans." Allison wanted to go with him, but she
knew he would not let her.

Drake went straight to the police station. Doug w
coming in first thing to identify Mr. Shannon as the man
who beat him up. Connor was coming in during his lunch
break. And Trenton was coming by after his morning
classes. Drake was sure they would get enough to book Mr.
Shannon on at least two charges of assault and battery. He
hoped to get a confession on the Landon murder as well.

Sergeant Michaels would agree to a plea bargain if Mr.
Shannon listed all his partners. Drake wasn't keen on the
idea but knew it may well be the only way to find out
whether or not Shannon was acting alone. Doug was sure
Shannon was the man who assaulted him in the parking lot.
After Doug confirmed Drake's suspicions, Drake had Doug
go with him to let Shannon know he had been positively
identified. He did the same thing with Connor and Trenton.

Mr. Shannon was officially charged, and given the
opportunity to rat on anyone who may be helping him.
Shannon was as cold as ice, straight faced, without anything
to say. If he had a partner, was working for someone, or
otherwise involved… he wasn't saying. Don't know why he
was watching Allison, why he was hurting her friends, or
what his end game was?

Drake and Detective Truman took search warrants
to the motel where Mr. Shannon had been staying. They
searched his room from top to bottom, tagging anything
and everything that might help in the case against him.
They also searched his car. They found addresses for Allison,
Madison, Mason, Trenton, and Connor. They also found
pictures of everyone. Drake caught the break he needed
when he found a picture of Taylor outside of Mason's house.

Finally, Mr. Shannon cracked after being charged with

..rder. He confessed and told them about everything ..fter being guaranteed a lesser sentence for helping to bring his accomplices in. Sergeant Michaels decided he did not want Allison to know anything else about the case, so she couldn't inadvertently give something away. Drake wasn't even allowed to tell her they were able to add another count of assault and battery to Mr. Shannon's record, after Tony Norman also identified him as his attacker.

Drake picked her up after work and filled her in, as much as he was allowed to anyway. He told her the case was not closed, and they were still investigating all of the leads. He reminded her not to speak to anyone about the case until he told her it was finally over. Drake and Allison stopped by the store on the way to her apartment. They agreed on roasted chicken and potato salad for supper, and apple pie for dessert. Drake knew Allison and Madison were contemplating going to the last Dillonsledge concert in California. After dinner, he told her he didn't think it would be a good idea to leave town right now, and asked if she thought Donovan would understand. "Besides, I'm not sure I trust you with a star of such caliber, if I can't be there to keep an eye on you."

Allison was surprised. "So does that mean you don't want me seeing other guys? And I should tell Donovan that I am seeing someone? I'm not sure I can do that unless I know that we are officially dating, which at the moment we can't be doing because the case isn't over yet. So technically, you can't even ask me out yet and I could still go to California and see Donovan and the last Dillonsledge concert."

"Technically, I guess you could." Drake got out of his chair, pulling her chair out. He bent down whispering in her

ear, rubbing his hands up and down her legs. "But wouldn't you rather date me?"

Allison shivered in her chair, squirming to get away. She pushed him away, sliding out of her chair and going over to the sink.

Drake followed her. He wrapped his arms around her, kissing the back of her neck. "I really don't want you seeing other guys, even if I can't technically ask you out yet."

"Who says you can't technically ask me out yet anyway? Is there a rule or something?" She turned around in his arms.

Drake moved his lips over hers. There was definitely a passion she couldn't feel with Donovan. "Ask me out now. Make me forget about Donovan."

Drake carried her to the bedroom. "So, this means we're not seeing other people, right? And I don't have to worry about you sneaking out to see the last concert?"

Allison slid his shirt off over his head. "Donovan who?"

Drake laughed. He took her hands in his, keeping her from running them over his chest. "I'm serious. I really like you, and I want us to start dating. Exclusively! Are you okay with that?"

She got serious, rolling over to her side. "I never thought of Donovan as anything more than my favorite band member. The sex was good, and I enjoyed his company, but I could never date him, or be anything more than friends... with benefits sometimes. But I liked you the first night you came to the apartment. The way you looked; the way you made me feel. I was so glad to see you at the station, even if you did have doubts about me being involved and you were just doing your job. I kind of got the idea that you might be

interested when you came by the night Camille was here, when we were baking. That is when I knew I wanted to get to know you better. I am more than okay with dating exclusively, and I can't wait until this is over. I am ready now!" She rolled back over pushing his shoulders down on the bed. "Are you sure about this?"

"Positively!" He reached over setting the alarm clock, and then pulled her down into his arms. Allison's phone rang. Drake let go so she could get up. "Are you going to get that?"

She snuggled into his comfortable arms, where she felt safe. "Nope! They can leave a message."

Chapter Twelve

Allison went to Shiley's Thursday morning with a new sense of security. She had no idea that Mr. Shannon was working on behalf of someone else. The only thing she knew was that Drake told her not to say a word about the investigation to anyone, until he told her she could. It was killing Allison to keep quiet. She knew when she called Donovan back it would be hard to tell him she was not going to be able to make it to the last concert. It would be even harder to tell him she was seeing someone now. Donovan had left three messages already, between last night and this morning. He called again before she got a chance to settle down at work and call him back. "Hello? I was going to call you as soon as I made rounds this morning. How was the show in LA?"

"It was all right. It could have been better, if I had seen the little hearts shining from out in the crowd." Donovan was teasing her.

"I know! I really wish we could make it out for the last show, but I am afraid we won't be able to. I can get off work, but Madison can't. And even if she could, I'm not able to leave right now." Allison knew she couldn't say anything about the case, but she needed to tell him about Drake.

"Is your family okay? Or what is wrong?" Donovan knew it had to be something big, to keep her away from a Dillonsledge concert.

Allison took a deep breath. "Donovan, there's something I have to tell you."

"I know, you're seeing someone."

Allison was shocked that he knew. "How'd you know that?"

There was a slight pause. "Derek told me. Madison said something earlier and Derek mentioned it to me. I wondered how long it would take you to tell me." Donovan already knew.

"I wanted to make sure we were really going to start seeing each other before I said something. I'm sorry." Allison considered going out for the last concert, but it would never be the same now.

"I understand. We had a fun time though. And I will miss being with you after the concerts. But you are still going to come to the concerts and bring the heart lights, aren't you? Even if you bring your new friend?"

Allison was relieved to know Donovan was cool with her seeing someone, and that he still wanted her to be friends. "He already said he wanted to come with me. If that's all right with you?"

"One more ticket sold! Of course, it is all right. Just do not forget to bring the key chains. So I guess that means I won't be coming out to see you after the tour is over?" Donovan laughed.

"You can come out if you want to. Derek is coming. And I'm sure there are plenty of girls around here that would love to keep you from being a fifth wheel."

"We will, see? I will probably pass this time, until I get the chance to see if me and your new beau get along. But thanks for the invite. And just in case things do not work out between the two of you, keep me in mind. I really like you, Allison. You are always welcome to join me on the road, anytime, anywhere. Remember that! Okay?"

"Thanks Donovan! I will remember. But I better let you go right now, or "G" will fire me. Let me know how the shows go tonight and tomorrow." Allison was glad to know telling Donovan about Drake went much smoother than she had thought it would. She really liked Donovan. He was such a good guy, but his lifestyle was so different, she knew she would never be able to get used to it. Allison was certain she had made the right decision about dating Drake.

She thought about Drake hard at work, catching bad guys, working on her case, trying to get it wrapped up. He told her it was coming along, and he hoped to get everything he needed by the end of the week, or the beginning of next week, but he wouldn't give her details.

Mr. Gillespie knocked on her opened door, teasing her to keep her mind on Shiley's. "You doin' okay in here? You know the guards are still here, so you do not have to worry. We have the new ad breaking Sunday that we need to concentrate on. I will be in my office waiting when you get ready. Take your time."

"Okay, I'll be there in a minute." Allison looked at the pictures around her office. She liked her life the way it was. She did not want it to change. She could not wait until Drake told her he had the whole Shannon thing taken care of. She could not help but wonder who he was and what he wanted from her. But she had work to do. She refused to let that criminal control any more of her thoughts. Allison and Mr. Gillespie spent the morning designing layouts for the sales items. After lunch, they moved racks to easy to find areas, and rearranged shelves putting all the sales items in easy to reach places.

Drake called late in the afternoon."Are you going to be able to go to Madison's after work? It is crazy busy here and I'm not going to be able to get away." He would be working late, on a new lead.

"I'm sure that won't be a problem. I'm sorry work is so busy right now, but if it's about my case, I hope that means you are close to figuring this out!" She was hoping for a little inside scoop.

"Nice try!" Drake laughed. "But that's not going to work."

"Well, you know what they say… You can't blame a girl for trying!" Allison called Madison and asked her if she wanted to go out for dinner after work and make sure it was okay to stay with her after. Madison agreed and told her she would be down to pick her up after work.

Allison and Mr. Gillespie finished checking the sales merchandise and getting the signs ready for the sale. They had just finished when Madison walked through. "Are you ready? Where would you like to go for dinner?" Madison had worked through lunch and was starting to get hungry.

"Perfect timing! We just finished here. Let me get my things and I'll be ready." Allison and Madison made their way up the stairs. "Is Rooster's, okay? Or would you rather go somewhere else?"

"Rooster's is fine."

Madison questioned Allison about Donovan's reaction

to the news, that they wouldn't be able to make it to the last show in California.

"I think he was more upset about that than he was at the fact that I was seeing someone." Allison seemed a bit puzzled.

"You told him about Drake?"

"I didn't have to. He already knew."

Madison was as shocked as Allison had been. "How did he know that?"

Allison did not think anything about it, and definitely didn't care if Madison said something to Derek about it. "He said Derek told him."

"How did Derek know?"

Now Allison was confused. "He said you said something to Derek and that Derek mentioned it to him! It is okay if you said something. I don't care."

"Thanks friend. I do appreciate that, but I didn't say anything to Derek. I swear!" Madison was more than sure that she hadn't said anything. "You know me, if it's not my story, I don't repeat it, or try to tell it. I was actually very careful about what I did say, so I wouldn't give it away. I didn't know if you wanted Donovan to know about Drake."

"I must have given him a clue or something without even realizing it. Or maybe he heard Drake in the background the other night when he called. I don't know. But why would he give me that whole spiel about Derek telling him? That doesn't make any sense."

"Do you remember exactly what he said?" Madison was concerned. "Maybe you should call Drake and tell him."

"Tell him what? That Donovan knew I was seeing someone before I told him."

"Drake did say that everyone was a suspect." Madison laughed.

"Maybe he was guessing, because I've been so distant lately." Allison didn't know, but she didn't care. He knew, and was okay with it, that's the only thing that mattered to her. Allison went to Madison's after they ate. They watched Dillonsledge videos and the concert from last year again.

Drake finally came by to pick Allison up. Madison told Drake about Donovan while Allison was in the bathroom. He made a note and said he would investigate it. That night, Allison was hoping Drake would tell her more about the case. He said they were getting close, and he would let her know when he could tell her everything. He did tell her that he had a very good day and things should be back to normal for her in just a couple of days. Drake felt sorry for her. He knew she was scared. But he could not tell her anything that might cause her to react differently and give something away.

They watched TV until it was time to go to bed. The following morning, Drake promised he would be able to tell her more tonight when he got home. He told her he wanted her to stay with Madison after work and that he would pick her up there tonight after he got back.

"Where are you going?" Allison figured it had something to do with her case and wanted to know what he was up to.

"You know I can't tell you that. But hopefully when I get back, this will all be over." That is all he would say. It was all Allison could do to keep her mind on her work. She checked the stockroom for more sales merchandise, making sure they had everything out.

Madison did not want to go to the food court for lunch,

so they had lunch in the break room. Trenton ate with them before he punched in. He wanted to know all about the case and was disappointed when Allison didn't really know anything to tell him. "But hopefully it will all be over with by tonight."

Donovan called that afternoon to tell her all about the show from the night before. "I can't believe tonight is the last show before we go to Europe. Have you ever been to Europe? You should take a vacation and go with us."

"You know I can't do that! I am seeing someone. Remember?"

"You still have a couple of weeks to think about it. You haven't been seeing him that long, have you? Let's see... Europe with me, or a new boyfriend that might not even last?" Donovan laughed. "I know you can't go, unless something happens between you and this new guy. Just promise me, you'll come back to me if he ever hurts you or breaks your heart."

"I don't think we'll have to worry about that. And even if I wasn't seeing someone, one week is not enough notice to take two weeks off. Mr. Gillespie would fire me before he let me have that much time off with such short notice."

"That would be okay too. Then you could just stay with me all of the time."

"Don't you have sound check or something you should be doing?" Allison changed the subject.

"And your lunch is almost over, so I should let you go."

Chapter Thirteen

Allison finished working and met Madison at Just Shoes. They grabbed dinner at a drive-thru and hurried home to watch the videos on the internet from the concert the night before. They loved the internet and all of the information they could get, and everything they could see without even being there. There were several videos posted from the night before already. Allison was horrified when she saw Mr. Shannon in the background talking to Donovan in one of the videos.

Madison told her Detective Truman and one of the other officers were using their tickets and backstage passes to get close to Donovan.

Allison stomped off. "What are you talking about?"

"Drake has new information that Mr. Shannon was following orders from Donovan."

"That's nonsense! Donovan would never do anything like that. Shannon is lying! This is going to hurt their career." Allison started crying.

Madison hugged her. "I wanted to tell you, but Drake wouldn't let me. He didn't want you to tip Donovan off.

Mr. Shannon agreed to help in the arrest of Donovan for a lesser sentence."

"See, he just wants a lighter sentence. He's lying." Allison refused to believe it. "I'm calling Donovan right now and clearing this up."

"I can't let you do that! Alli I have heard the tape. He's guilty, and now we just need better evidence." Madison shook her head. "I know it's hard to believe, but Donovan wanted you all to himself and he was going to do whatever it took to make it happen."

"That's just not true! It can't be. Tape? What tape are you talking about? What tape did you hear?" Allison sat down.

Madison sat down beside her. "Drake had me come down to the station this morning. He told me Shannon agreed to turn his accomplice in and that he might need my help. He let me listen to the recorded phone conversation between Shannon and Donovan. Donovan admitted to wanting Drake dead."

Allison almost threw up! "Are we sure it was Donovan he was talking to?"

"It was Donovan! I am sorry! Mr. Shannon and the two officers flew out yesterday afternoon to confront Donovan. They are working with the California sheriff's department. Drake was going to go, but Sergeant Michaels said he was too close to the case. The Sergeant did not tell Drake he was sending the others early, without him! He didn't find out until he got to the station this morning."

"That's what he was talking about when he said something about getting back. He thought he was going this morning." Allison looked around for her handbag.

"So where is Drake now?"

"I imagine he's still at the station."

Allison called him. Drake answered on the first ring. "Drake, I have to tell you something. Donovan knew I was seeing someone before I told him. And he lied about Derek telling him because Madison said she never said anything to Derek. And just now, we saw video footage from the concert last night; Shannon is in the background talking to Donovan."

Drake could not get a word in. He finally told her to come down to the station and he would fill her in, if Sergeant Michaels said it was all right. Madison drove as quickly as she could without getting a ticket. Drake was waiting for them when they got there. He showed them all of the evidence and told them what Detectives Truman and Garcia were doing. "Mr. Shannon was wearing a wire and confronted Donovan the night before. Donovan admitted that he wanted me dead, and out of your life permanently. We decided to send Shannon back to try and get Donovan to say something about the payment for killing Mr. Landon. They are going to arrest Donovan first thing after the concert is over, if they get what they need."

Allison was numb. No tears. No more fears. She felt nothing. She just sat there. Drake apologized and said he would give her time to take it all in. He went out to speak with Sergeant Michaels. Sergeant Michaels came in and apologized for treating her like a suspect earlier in the case.

"That's okay. I understand why you would think such a thing. Is there any way we may be wrong about Donovan?"

"I'm afraid we have all of the evidence we need to put him away for a long time. The only thing we do not have is a confession about the earlier beatings and the death of Mr. Landon, which we are hoping to get as soon as the concert is over tonight. I am sorry, Ms. Drexler. Ms. Cannon." The Sergeant left the room.

Allison finally started crying. "Everyone is going to hate me. All the fans are going to blame me. Because you know everyone is going to find out about this, then they will hate me. Some of them will probably even try to hurt me. My life as we know it is over. I will probably be in more danger now than I was before!"

Drake assured her they were going to keep this as quiet as possible and that her real name would not be used. So no one would know it was her, and she would be fine.

Allison laughed. "You grossly underestimate the fortitude of devoted fans. They will find out! The boys always tease about how the fans always know everything." She kept talking. Madison took her hand, shaking her head.

"Okay. I don't fully get it. But it is late, and you need to get out of here." He tried to get them to go back to Madison's, but Allison said she wasn't leaving Drake's side. "Not now, not ever!"

"Fair enough! But at least try to get some rest" He kissed her on the top of the head and turned the lights down as he left to get them something to drink.

Derek was the first one to call. He gave Madison a play by play of the situation. "Oh my God, you were right. They just arrested Donovan. That Shannon guy got him to talk. Then Donovan knocked him out and was beating him. I do not think he would have stopped either. Those detectives stopped him. Donovan tried saying Shannon was a stalker and that he had attacked him, and that he was defending himself. The officers told him Mr. Shannon was wearing a wire and that they knew the truth. They read him his rights and cuffed him out by the buses."

"Are you still flying in tomorrow?" Madison did not know if Derek was still going to try to come see her.

"I think I'm going home first, see the parents, let them know I'm all right. I'll fly in Monday or Tuesday. Is that all right?"

"That's fine Derek. And I'll even understand if you don't want to see me anymore."

"Well why wouldn't I want to see you? You didn't have anything to do with all of this. It is Allison who may not want to see me.

"She doesn't hold this against any of you. She feels really bad though, and blames herself."

"I'll just call mom and dad to let them know everything is okay, and fly out to you later today! Because Allison needs to know we don't blame her and that none of this is her fault. Tell her I'll see her later." Before he hung up, he surprised her. "Hey Madison, maybe this way, when I do go see the folks, you'll be able to go with me?"

Drake was busy getting all the details from the Sergeant. They were flying Donovan back to Florida tonight. He would be charged and tried where the assaults took place. He didn't have a leg to stand on with the recorded phone conversations and the recorded confession of paying Shannon to keep everyone away from Allison; Donovan would be found guilty.

Drake finally talked Allison into staying at Madison's all night. "You'll have a long day ahead of you, so you need to get a good night's sleep."

"What about you?"

"I still have all of this paperwork to finish before they get back. I want it to be done and be ready to go when they get here. I'll go home as soon as I finish."

Dreams can be cruel. What once was so sweet and welcoming during sleep now haunted her. Allison tossed and turned dreaming of a man she could honestly say she loved, even though she knew from the beginning she would never be able to leave her life or her reality for. Dreams? Donovan wanted her. She seriously considered it… life, with Donovan. But no, she couldn't. All the time… Donovan wanted her. All to himself. Dreams? Why? No! Don't hurt him! She'd leave her life, her reality, all for Donovan. Never! The fans. Oh no, the fans too? No don't hurt me! Nightmares! Donovan wanted her. He made sure he had her. All to himself. Taunting. So possessive. Shackles? "Nnnoooooooooo!" Allison woke up screaming. Soaking wet with sweat. She stripped on the way to the shower. Bawling.

Madison ran in to check on her friend. She hadn't slept yet, because she could not stop crying. For her friend. For her boyfriend. For herself. For the rest of the boys. She adjusted the temperature of the water and joined her friend.

Derek called a few hours later. He had flown in last night with Donovan and the officers. The girls got dressed and swung by to get coffee and pastries on their way to the station. Derek ran up and bear-hugged Allison. He told her he was sorry for what Donovan had done to her and all her friends. "None of this is your fault. We don't blame you for Donovan's actions, and you shouldn't blame yourself either."

Drake confirmed what Derek had told Madison in

the phone call... Donovan was behind it all and had been arrested. "Allison, Donovan wants to see you. He said he wants to see you first and then Dillon; and then he will confess." Drake told her she didn't have to see him if she didn't want to. But Allison wanted to see him. She loved him, that just doesn't go away. She thought seeing him would somehow make it easier to put it all behind her.

"Fine, but I'm going in there with you. You are not going in there by yourself."

"He had pictures of you, Drake. He wanted you dead because of me. You are not going in there with me!"

She said she would only go in if Derek would go with her. Derek agreed. Allison was holding Derek's hand as they walked into the interrogation room. Detective Truman was standing on the other side of the room, behind Donovan. She did not say anything but nodded. Donovan started crying. Detective Truman reminded him that everything he said was being recorded. She had Allison and Derek state their names for the record.

Donovan apologized to Derek. "Tell the guys I'm sorry!" Derek told him Dillon and Dominic went home, that they were not coming to see him. "I don't blame them. I blew it for the whole group. I really am sorry Derek."

Allison started to cry. "Why Donovan? Why did you do it? You did not have to do it! I loved you. They were nothing but friends, or even less than friends. You hurt them for nothing, Donovan. You ruined it and hurt all of those people for nothing!"

"I don't know what happened; I just wanted you all to myself. I love you so much Allison. I love you. Please forgive me. I know we can make this work out."

Allison shook her head. "You didn't have to do any of this." She turned to leave.

"Don't go Allison. I love you. Allison? We can make this work!" Derek pulled the door shut behind them.

Drake was waiting right outside the door. He put his arm around her to help hold her up. "I'm sorry Allison! I shouldn't have let you go in there."

"It's okay. So how much longer are you going to be here?"

"I'm done with all of my paperwork. Truman and Garcia have to finish their reports and the rest is up to the attorneys."

Sergeant Michaels told them thank you and said he would be contacting them if they had any more questions. "Good work, Larson."

"Thanks, Sarge! So, am I free to go?"

"Yep. The rest of the weekend is yours for the taking."

"Did you hear that? So where do we want to go?" Drake asked Madison if she had anything in mind for Derek.

"I hadn't even thought about it yet, to be perfectly honest with you." Madison shrugged her shoulders.

"All right then, I know the perfect place! I'll drive." Drake led them to his car.

"So where are you taking us?" Allison wanted to know.

"You'll see!" Madison and Derek were talking the whole time, not really paying any attention to where they were going. Allison asked him if he was going to the mall.

"I thought Derek might like to see where Madison works."

"That's perfect! Thanks Drake." Work was the only

place Madison had thought about maybe taking Derek so far, so this turned out to be the best spot possible.

Drake parked the car and locked the doors. He held Allison's hand as they walked into the mall. He stopped outside the main entrance.

Allison gave him a funny look. "What's wrong?"

"Nothing! There's something I have to ask you."

"What?" Allison thought it had to do with the case. "Allison Drexler, will you go out with me?"

She playfully slapped him across the arm. "What? I thought we already had that settled."

"We did, kinda. But it is official now. The case is closed. We have the bad guy. It is over. I can ask you now. So, I am asking. Allison Drexler, will you go out with me? Exclusively? Just you and me?"

Allison jumped into his arms. "Yes Drake Larson, I will go out with you." She kissed him, and whispered in his ear. "Thank you, Drake. For everything. I couldn't have gotten through this without you."

"You're welcome! Now let's go have that first date! And I'm ordering for you." They walked into the mall.

"Oh really?"

"Yep! Fish, potatoes, and bananas!"

Derek shivered. "Yuck! Bananas, with fish and potatoes."

Allison and Drake explained on their way to the food court.

"Oh! In that case, make it two!"

"Three!" Madison would have the same thing.

Drake said they might as well make it four. "I'll get the fish sandwiches."

Allison said she would get the loaded baked potatoes.

Madison said she would get the banana smoothies.

Derek felt left out. "What do I get to get?"

"Me!" Madison took his arm in hers and dragged him toward the smoothie counter. "You can help me carry the smoothies."

"Okay! But tonight, I am taking all of us out for dinner!" Derek kissed Madison. "How do you think Allison is doing? Really doing?"

"I think she is doing all right. She will be fine. Drake will see to that."

"Good! I like Drake. I'm glad Alli has him."

"Me too, Derek!" They watched Drake and Allison making eyes at each other across the food court. Madison quietly whispered to herself. "Me too, Derek. Me too."

Derek laughed. "So do you know if he plays the guitar, or sings?"

About the Author

Bad luck with love and all, I am a sucker for true love and faithfully remain a hopeless romantic. Hi, my name is Jennifer Lee Burns. I was blessed to be given writing as an outlet at a very young age in my life. I remember sitting at the piano writing my little songs and poems, so many poems.

Much later, I started my first children's book one night – after getting off work at midnight, driving home, I got the idea; so I pulled off onto the side of the road, and began writing (the only thing I had to write on was napkins.)

When it comes to matters of the heart, I have it covered… literally. I've worked in the Cardiac ICU and the Open Heart ICU, and worked in Florida as a Cardiac Monitor Tech where I watched heart rhythms all night. However, I am back in Indiana now with my mom and our dog Dolly, and I am able to concentrate on writing full time for the first time. I am glad to say I am happier now than I have ever been, and excited to finally be sharing my books with you. I've laughed and cried creating the characters in my books. I hope you get invested enough in their stories, so you also feel the emotions they go through living on each page.

Printed in the United States
by Baker & Taylor Publisher Services